Bringing in the Creeps

Ray Van Horn, Jr

Anuci Press

Copyright © 2025 by Ray Van Horn, Jr

rvanhornjr@gmail.com

First paperback edition 2025

Anuci Press edition 2025

www.anuci-press.com

Cover Design by Matt Slay

Wrap Assembled by Adrian Medina

ISBN 979-8-9926529-4-9 (paperback)

ISBN 979-8-9926529-5-6(eBook)

BRINGING IN THE CREEPS

BRINGING IN THE CREEPS

Short Fiction by Ray Van Horn, Jr.

For Paulette, my first friend coming out of the womb.

Dealer of my annual King fixes since 1983, the stories of my life which gave birth to these tales of terror.

Much love to you and Mark. Friendship is forever.

Table of Contents

End of Midway — 4

Galaga Dreams — 18

Age of Quarrel — 22

Wolf Con — 38

The Cleansing of the Soles — 54

The Equine of Loch Raven — 57

Run — 75

Chickeerun — 93

Lucky Burns — 118

Widow — 133

Meteor Shit — 166

Author's Note — 194

End of the Midway

It came to me yesterday, gore slung, shredded, redder than the last time I'd seen such intense viscera.

Not a mere announcing *it* was back, but an invitation. A challenge. A goddamn ultimatum.

My neighbors' cat, Penelope (a name I thought was cute, if outdated, the kind of name tagged by hopeless romantics) was left strewn upon my deck. In pieces, intestines and organs encumbering the recent power washed slats. Fur and slaughter stained the one place left in this life I considered sanctum. The monster knew its business. It knew where and how to get to me. I mean really *get* to me.

And here I thought the twisted, scaly, toothy son of a bitch was dead.

I should know, since I, with some assistance, blew the fucker apart back in 1999 after it had tormented the woods outside the Reese firemen's carnival grounds the same year. Disappearances of livestock, a pig, two cows and a horse, plus three humans, one of them a six-year-old boy, had shocked rural Reese out of its farm boy britches. Two of those people were my wife, Christine, and our son, Simon. Simon, being the six-year-old boy.

The town of Reese never knew, never saw what had taken those lives. I'm glad about that. The funeral for town planner Jed McGee had gained public attention from the regional newspapers and the Baltimore t.v. news stations. Nobody outside the *Carroll County Times* had bothered to report the deaths of Christine and Simon.

I buried my family in the company of her parents, cousins and one surviving aunt, Bonnie. None of whom have talked to me since. Like they blame me or at least hate me for being unable to prevent Christine's death. A few of Simon's preschool teachers showed, which was nice. The whole farewell felt miniscule for what was the most torturous moment of my existence. Miniscule save for the burial fees.

How do you downplay such brutality when served upon you by a crusty-faced monstrosity with choppers dangling so low yet so wide, it's hard not to think God screwed up one day and kicked His mis-evolution to the curb with a purposefully obtuse walk amongst the clouds? No doubt whistling "Bringing in the Sheaves" while doing so.

I always feel the world open beneath me whenever I remember the unholy vision of Christine and Simon's mangled remains at the Carroll County Coroner's office. You never forget the outrage of seeing pummeled, lifeless bodies you're forced beyond your endurance to identify. One you married and one you made in union.

The only comfort I took until yesterday was I had tracked the hard-to-find beast down with our former town sheriff, Hank Lewiston, and blew it back to God where it belonged.

Like Depeche Mode once sang, though, God tends to have a sick sense of humor, because the beast is back, and it has a bloody reckoning in mind.

I don't have the heart to tell my hopeless romantic neighbors, Bob and Linda, their beloved Penelope ran afoul of a behemoth they missed the first time more than two decades ago. A behemoth that's supposed to be dead but took its grievances against me out on their pet calico.

It took everything I had not to toss my cookies while cleaning up Penelope's remains. I cried while hosing off the deck, thinking about what that awful thing did to Christine and Simon. Gnashed my teeth in a rage sweeping myself back to the coroner's office to recall their slashed and spread open corpses. I'd wanted revenge and took it. Sheriff Lewiston is the only one who can back that entire saga up.

The beast is now the one who's come calling for vengeance. Unlike 1999 where it had taken me and Lewiston more than a month of covert searching beneath Reese's purposeful tunnel vision, I knew damn well where to find it.

I'm scared out of my mind, but there's a pistol tucked overtop my manhood and a harnessed bowie knife strapped to my right thigh beneath a pair of ratty, ancient cargo shorts I need a belt these days to keep up. Christine hated these shorts when she was alive, saying they made me look fat. I'd defiantly held onto them, stashed into the furthest corner of my lowest dresser drawer. Unknowing, 20 pounds lighter, they'd be called upon to serve a higher purpose.

I can smell the carnival cuisine from the grassy knolls of the annex parking across the firehouse. The popcorn, as desiccated as the arid sky above. The cotton candy, always a guarantee to leave colored sugar trails beneath untrimmed fingernails.

Used to be I'd come to Reese carnival just for the pit beef. That was after one ride too many on The Zipper when the helter skelter ride broke before my wife, Christine, who threatened to leave me after ten minutes being hung upside down. Neither of us expected her to really leave one day.

I wonder if today's my own last day in this hellhole.

I expect so, if I'm going to be honest.

I haven't been to the carnival in years, not since Christine and I took Simon when he was six. Our boy's maiden spin on the Ferris Wheel. Simon had clung to Christine for dear life on the slow rise and halt as the ride operators shuttled people on and off. Once we were revolving in gentle tandem to the appositely crushing detonation of Metallica's "Enter Sandman" from the far more chaotic Himalaya ride below, Simon relaxed. I remember his marveling at the sights from up high, especially the birds swooping by in circular confusion finding humans on their level. Chirping amongst themselves their equivalent of "WTF?"

Thinking about it gives me strength. I can only hope I'm wearing more of the beast's blood than my own when tonight is done.

A family with three girls and a lone boy who looks lost in the shuffle skitter by me. The boy looks up at me warily, toting that hangdog expression anyone who feels anonymous would.

"'scuse me," he says, dodging my crinkled and cruddy Addidas sneaker which could easily take the abuse. Considering I've owned these shoes for nearly a decade, there's zilch in the way of resale value. Hell, I'm probably about to end up at the Carroll County Coroner in them tonight with far worse than crinkles and crud.

"Quite alright, my man," I say back to him. It's caught by the parents, not the sisters, who are in their own world yammering about kettle cakes and what I can only assume is popular tween anime. They're fawning over a shared adoration of someone called Chika Fujiwara. The parents give me an approving smile, which I return but don't feel. I'm jealous as hell.

I let the family drift away and hold my spot for a moment, inhaling the freshly cut grass serving as the impromptu parking lot, along with the enticing aromas from the carnival grounds. The pit beef will have to hold, though sweet potato fries sound incredible right now.

The mid-July sun has nearly finished its exodus, leaving a maroon pink spread along the horizon. It looks like a sanguinary prophecy.

"Yo, Mikey!" I hear from inside the Reese firehouse. From a guy I graduated high school with a lifetime ago, Kenny Rill. We'd partied together and raised some hell during those rambunctious days of rad. Busting beer bottles in driveways, unearthing mailboxes and ditching them blocks away. Dumb young guy shit.

Kenny was leaning against a galvanized pole planted between a vibrant red water tender and pumping truck. He was holding a dinnertime cup of Dunkin' and dumped into relaxed baggy jeans plus a once-white tee with a vanishing gold "ENGINE HOUSE 86" insignia plastered above his flaccid chest. A walking metaphor spiking our inevitable fadeout as a generation.

"Yo!" I shout back without losing my stride. I was in no mood to reminiscence about days filled with poached Coors, *Friday the 13th* films and beat-up Corvettes we were too ass-broke to upgrade. It's probably the last we'll see of each other, and I'm not up for goodbyes.

Entering the carnival midway, I'm greeted by the peppy country stylings of Chris Stapleton, music that's take it or leave it with me since I'm forever hung on Eighties thrash metal. Here in Reese, country music is nearly as king as Jesus Christ, the twanging nexus uniting inveterate good 'ol boys and the tenderfoot middle class transplants.

An immediate haze trails into my face like foggy ether in one of those British horror flicks which used to creep Christine out. A combined sinew of raised up dirt and clouds from the nearby barbecue pit, which the local Teamsters and off-duty firemen work. A twelve-person deep line is already loaded in queue.

It smells so damn good, but my appetite is appropriately quashed thinking about the woods pitched off the carnival grounds, where I'd first found the creature's den of slung entrails, severed heads and limbs torn with gristle hanging off. Puke inducing stuff that's hilarious in metal music lyrics, but shit-inducing *fear* to see in the real.

It happened here at Reese Carnival in 1999.

I'm feeling clammy by the recollection of it, though it could be natural perspiration from the summer hangover.

I see a few faces I know down the promenade, many I don't. Everything's ringing, joinging and gaffing from the game hucksters. One poor chump who lost at the bucket and ball stirs up a clem amidst the carny's continued grind for new suckers for their tawdry stuffed animals and cheap painted mirrors. Harried parents are counting their ticket ducats under duress from the insurrection of their unrelenting kids.

Business as usual.

I feel seething inside my guts. Hatred of the monster. Envy of everyone else, who yet again has no clue what evil looks like, even in its proverbial back yard. Reese's population is a mere 359. It's a wonder I'm the only one who knows what's about to happen if I don't take a stand.

Again.

Knowing what's hiding in the woods, past the Scrambler at the end of the midway, I still wince to see the trees have risen higher and thickened out since I last ventured into them.

Call it kismet. I call it more of God's sick sense of humor, or perhaps His grand design to align the same players, since His royal fuckup appears to have conjoined with the devil for a bloody resurrection.

I come across none other than Sheriff Hank Lewiston, who held watch over Reese for nearly thirty years before retiring. He'd busted me twice in my balls-aching younger years for pot possession. When you could do a little time in the pokey for all that tokey. We're good, though, as you'd probably guess. Long good.

Sheriff Lewiston's not getting around as readily as he once did, plodding with a walker, flanked by his two overgrown grandsons who look shamefully inconvenienced helping the former town guardian along.

"Michael," Lewiston calls to me with a babble indicating he may be destined for a harder road than Buckey's Mill, which hasn't been repaved in more than two decades.

"Sheriff," I return to him with a tender wave. Those who've lived in Reese long enough address him the same.

We both look at one another for a fleeting second, since Sheriff Lewiston was there in '99 when the carnage flung and the abomination which had done it was put down. So he and I had thought.

An abomination which has astoundingly returned to Reese.

"You're not here to ride the Tilt-a-Whirl, I take it?" Lewiston quips, halting his walker. His lineage looks downright put-out, and I want to Moe-smack them in one swipe. If they only knew.

"Afraid not," I answer in a flat monotone. Our former Sheriff may be long in the tooth, but he catches on immediately.

"Oh, dear God," Lewiston says, struggling to straighten up, as if Youth Springs Eternal was cruelly enticing him with false seduction of sweeping him back to his lean and muscular 1999 body. "You've informed Sheriff Gaines, I hope?"

"No," I mumble, feeling sour from the admission, but also from the way Lewiston's lousy grandsons could give a shit less what we're saying, much less their elder's sudden blanch and noticeable quivering. Porky, uncaring assholes.

"H-how do you know?" Lewiston stutters. Having had a stroke two years ago, he's one rocky step from full-time palsy.

"There was a present left on my deck," I tell him, rubbing my abdomen.

Unneeded code there's a stashed loaded gun there.

"Animal or otherwise?" Lewiston asks with another tremble. Now his grandsons have become invested.

"The hell's he going on about?" Grandson 1 on Lewiston's left grumbles at me. Earl is the kid's name. Grandson 2 on the right is Spencer. Spencer obviously idolizes fishing icon Bill Dance enough to wear the man's corporate sponsored shirt sporting a bloated bass caricature. Earl would be a kid after my own heart if he wasn't an ungrateful shit towards his grandfather, since he's got a tent of a tee yielding a crimson logo from the *Saw* movies.

"My neighbors' calico, Penelope," I tell Sheriff Lewiston, giving Ernie no further thought other than thinking he'd epic fail at one of Jigsaw's gory trap games. "A hot mess, exactly as you'd remember it, Sheriff."

"Christ," Lewiston snarls now, and I admire his sudden moxy. "Gaines needs to know."

"I'd consider it a favor if he didn't," I tell Lewiston with a calm planting of my hand upon his rubbery, diminished shoulder. It breaks my heart to feel anything other than chiseled bone and musculature from the old days. "I got this."

"Damn if you don't, son," Lewiston says to me like I'm the only one on the carnival grounds. Like there are no kids screeching down the wavy iron slides on those burlap sacks which trail at the end, leaving brush burns. Like there's no clusters of teenagers looking at their cell phones more than each other while bumping into their elders without excusing themselves.

"It's gotta be done," I blurt, keeping the second weapon on me a secret. "You know this."

"Grandpa?" Spencer blurts, shifting his eyes between me and his senior, whom I know would soon kick his walker into the next town, Hamilton, if he could manage it and accompany me into the woods. Just as he did in 1999.

"You be careful, Michael," Lewiston heaves with a phlegm-clogged sigh as I release his sagging shoulder. "Don't know when the good Lord's gonna come calling for me, but I hope to see you again before that happens."

"Yes, sir," I say, giving him a wink. "You just may, or I may catch you on the other side. I kinda hope for the second scenario. You understand."

"I'd call you a goddamn fool, but that would make me a hypocrite," Lewiston grumbles, leaning into his walker. "Take me home, boys. I've lost my appetite for those Italian sausages. Just as well, since they always give me the runs."

Ernie appears like he wants to throttle me as much as get answers to some suspicious shit he's been exposed to. I quietly hum those daunting, expository chimes during the big reveal at the end of each *Saw* movie. It's more a defense mechanism than a razz. The scabby, ugly entity's back and it wants to play a game I don't think I'll win.

It's Spencer who says something, and I unexpectedly grimace from it.

"I figured Grandpa's been off his rocker all this time talking about that monster stuff. You're telling me it's real."

I give Spencer the faintest of nods as I turn away and lose myself into a crowd of people just leaving the Bingo pavilion, half of them grinning, half of them looking like their entire night's been shat upon.

Later, I'm stashed inside the woods, watching the last round of people glide through the night air on the Chair-o-Planes. The ride's shutdown lags the Scrambler and the Dodgem bumper cars, but the midway empties in much faster time than I expect. Enough for me to spot cloud emissions belching overtop the teenaged ride operators, toking on ganja like Kenny and I did at their hurry-to-grow-up ages.

I've been holding this spot for nearly three hours, screened by hardwood buffers with very little spatial patterns to worry about. Conifers, oaks, maples and ash have swallowed my vantage yet giving me enough of a glimpse to make sure everyone's packing up.

The woods are also harboring *it,* and I know it's somewhere behind me. Close, far away. That, I don't know. These woods, according to Carroll County mapping, are more than two miles long before pitching out onto Old Westminster Pike where Reese confluences with Finksburg.

I only know it's been waiting for the same reason. For fewer people to witness what will turn into a blood spectacle.

"I'd say welcome back, you gruesome bastard," I mutter. "But you were never welcome in the first place, especially taking it out on that poor cat just to get my attention. This is for her and my wife and kid. A second time."

I needn't say anything else.

I feel hot combustion before I hear the spit-slung snorting. There's very little light, save for the quarter crescent peeking through the upwards foliage and the dimmed track lighting from the carnival grounds. The midway suddenly seems miles away.

I whip out my Hi-Point C9 from where it's stored above my crotch. I thumb the safety loose and fire. Not once or twice, but four times, half of the magazine. The nine-millimeter polymer pumps my palm like it's missed me all these years.

I hit true, just as Sheriff Lewiston and I did in 1999.

An agonizing yowl pierces my ears, louder than standing next to Motorhead's Marshall SuperBass amp at Ozzfest '98 without ear plugs. The pain is just the same and my ear canals hint at turning deaf forever to the battle's din.

My pistol's swatted away, my right hand nearly with it. Talons I'm familiar with dig into my wrist so deep I initially think it's been severed. I may have gotten first blood, but the monster's drawn *worse* blood. I feel the gush and hear my essence spatter sickeningly upon the ground before I'm shoved backwards.

The flash of trees and stars look beautiful, but they're a temporary reprieve as the view is snatched by the repugnant rictus of spiked teeth which stink something awful. Like the thing had eaten a bowl of rotten hard-boiled eggs and something fleshier for dessert.

I hear the nauseating chomp into my left collar bone before I feel it. When my motor senses catch up, that's when I scream, hardly worried about who's left to alarm at the carnival. Hell, as if my gunshots hadn't caused enough of a stir. All that stealth for *this* madness louder than Motorhead's most debilitating decibels.

"No," I whisper-gurgle, as I hear a group of people clambering towards the woods, shouting man-mongrel offerings of help. My throat is already soaked, and it tastes like weak rum. I'm every bit the goddamned fool Lewiston said I was. The thing called me out, though. What else was I supposed to do?

The thing chews deeper into my jugular, and I gasp as my hollering tails off. Yet I command my right hip to endure the punishment from the other side and hoist my knee so I can pull up my shorts and unsheathe my knife. My labored lurching makes the pain even more terrible.

The next sequence of events goes in such a blur I barely realized I've planted my knife into the thing's foul, encrusted temple.

It howls louder than I did, our chorus of anguish joined by a litany of expletives from do-gooders who I try like hell to warn from coming any further. I get nothing out through the choke of my pooling blood, save for a wretched cough of spew.

The outer edge of the woods is suddenly washed with spinning red and blue lights.

"Jesus wept!" I hear before a flurry of gunfire shreds the thing, pushing it off me, blowing most of its leprous right cheek off.

The rematch with this horrible miscreation, much like the first, except I'm going to die this time. It's a certainty. Like Christine could make me holler like a Viking when we made love by tickling me *there* and clenching on my shudder. Like Simon could always make me laugh screwing up the alphabet he was still learning at the time of his brutal death. I hear it now above the gunfire and monstrous bellowing: *"A-G-P-K-F-C..."*

The creature bafflingly hangs in there and I grunt from the awful sensation of sharp, bony nails sinking and tugging into my intestines.

I can't get air between my severed, squirting neck and now my extracted abdomen.

At least I got the fucking thing. Again.

"There's a man down there, Sheriff!" I detect, knowing it's not Lewiston being addressed, but our current sentinel, Gaines.

Gaines confirms his presence by barking back, "I see him, dammit!"

More gunfire and the beast's finally out of my life for good.

This final shot, double the volume from a sawed-off, and I see a fountain of blood and brains erupt like phantasmagoria, spotlighted in midair from whisking flashlights—freakish splatter art.

Voices parade behind the spectacle. A couple I know. Others, total strangers.

"Where are the medics, for Christ's sake? We're gonna lose him!"

"Hey, isn't that Mike Harig, the guy who lost his wife and kid all those years ago?"

"Shut up, Phil, don't you have any fucking couth? The poor bastard's about to join them! Christ, look at the sight of him!"

"Sheriff!" I hear, knowing I'm not far from checking out, happy for it, knowing it's all done, even as someone flops to the ground with a heaving groan next to me, pressing a balled-up shirt against my neck. A pointless gesture, if comforting. I'm bleeding out from my stomach equally fast.

It's Ernie, now a shirtless glob of flesh, but for the first time since I met him, he sounds like he honestly gives a damn as he orders his brother to check on their grandfather.

"Grandpa doesn't have a pulse!" Spencer shrieks. "He needs help, oh, my God! Grandpa! I'm sorry I always called you all those names! It *was* real!"

I wish I could see Lewiston in the back of Gaines' cruiser since I know that's where he is. Just so we could smile one last time together. My cavalry for one last glory ride. We did it. One more time. Hopefully the last.

I pray for the last time. Pray God's done pushing his dirty work upon His beloved makings.

"Race you there, old man," I squib through my last bloody breath, already seeing my boy clapping at me like he did after that first Ferris Wheel ride.

Galaga Dreams

1982.

She was wearing Calvin Klein, though I was more of a Jordache guy. Not that it mattered. Holly Kolakowski could make bargain rack Levi dungarees a denim billboard of sin the way she rocked her lean hips and trim ass, thrusting her crotch at video game machines. She conquered them like older ladies did with men.

Playing Galaga and Time Pilot, Holly was clothed amateur porn when she had her fist clenched upon a joystick and her rightward middle three fingers pounding fire buttons. She'd made Galaga her bitch and seldom few got their turns if she'd claimed the alien shooting game first.

Holly Kolakowski was hardly my crush. That was Jeannie Maser, who didn't know I existed, even having three classes together.

Holly was dropping the equivalent of a hate fuck upon the Dig Dug machine, of all low-stress games. Her toned buttocks were clenching and grinding, putting on a hell of a show for the lookee-loos.

By the time I said what I had to say to Holly, the show would be over.

One of us would be gone for good.

Space Port was popping tonight, for a Thursday. The neon piping broke into the dimly lit fugue of the arcade, reminding me of *Tron*. The movie, of course, since the way-too-easy game had laid like a wet fart without the roast to check oneself. The *Tron* machine stood there right now, unwanted, like a lone, greasy spaz at Prom Night.

The orchestra of electric mayhem in the way of bleeps, doops, zaps and artificial detonation was supplemented by jangles of the dollar changer machines and Journey's "Don't Stop Believin'" waxing overhead. The song had already become a cliché for me.

The murkiest part of Space Port, between other shunned games like Pengo and Xevious was a crevice just enough for two people to squeeze into. Amongst us kids, it was called "The Makeout Zone." Right now, occupied by Keith Shaw and Valerie Spinelli. They were going at it hot, to the point Keith went for the hooter honk in plain view and Valerie didn't check him for it.

"Get bent," Valerie snarled at me as I lingered too long watching them.

"The looks of things, I'm not the one getting bent tonight," I sent back with the same smartass tongue my parents warned would get my duff kicked one day. Val snickered at my jibe. Keith flipped me off.

Holly was hammering the pump action button on Dig Dug so hard I'm surprised she didn't sprain her wrist. Not fast enough, however, as she was gobbled by one of those weird, bloated ghost things wearing what looked like ski goggles.

Game over.

"Holly," I said, feeling provocation rise inside my throat.

"The hell do you want, Ricky Lowe?" she sassed with a whirl from the machine. "Got a quarter? I'm out."

"No," I said flatly, a total lie since I still had seventy-five cents inside my pocket.

"Then take a hike, already," she said with more dismissal than Rhett Butler's brutal parting shot to Scarlett O'Hara.

"I just want you to know, Holly," I said, looking into hazel eyes now darting around nervously. Murderer's eyes. "I know what you did."

"Say what?" she hissed, taking a step away from me.

I took the same step, blocking her path.

"I know."

"You don't know shit," she growled, guilt flashing across her face. The gleam of an unoccupied Missile Command machine accented her culpability. "Whatever it is you think I did."

"Two words for you," I said confidently, again stepping into Holly's path.

"Out of my way, Ricky, before I kill you," she fumed, clenching both fists.

Now I had her.

"Like you did to Wayne Reynolds. Well, that was six words, but whatever."

If a girl could go paler than a winter whiteout, that's how Holly looked, even with aquamarine, yellow and ultraviolet flushes slashing her liable face.

It was a wild card play, but last night my curiosity was up. I'd found a watermelon Bubblicious gum wrapper at the crime scene where Wayne Reynolds' brains had been bashed out with a hammer. No prints detected. Holly'd had enough savvy to wear gloves.

Wayne once bragged to me in the locker room he'd kissed Holly underneath the visiting side bleachers on the football field. He'd said her breath was "rancid from that stupid watermelon gum."

Why Holly had killed Wayne, I didn't know.

All I do know is the following morning, the cops had their girl.

Age of Quarrel

It was a night the Cro Mags were supposed to be playing, but an unexpected cancelation from bassist/vocalist Harley Flanagan meant we got Dirty Trace as the headliners that night. Pale shade mimics of their DC straight edge brethren Minor Threat, who'd long given up the fight.

I'd been at The Black Tarot the week prior when Agnostic Front and Verbal Assault peeled the paint off the three-year-old nightclub which had been converted from a short-lived gay singles bar formerly called Unity. The mosh pit had been revved all night long. I was still carrying a few bruises to prove it.

The Black Tarot had been booking more metal, thrash and industrial bands than punk and hardcore. Hence, more of those types were attending our shows. The age of crossover has arrived, with Suicidal Tendencies, D.R.I. and the Crumbsuckers having gone speed metal.

I was there the night Dirty Trace had worse things to worry about than being razzed by a thinned-down crowd barking call-to-arms lyrics of the Cro Mags' stomp anthem, "We Gotta Know" while they were setting up their gear onstage. My late buddy, Greg King, went so far as to wear his faded *Age of Quarrel* t-shirt to the gig in protest. Greg wore that damn Cro Mags shirt so often I once joked he'd probably be buried in it one day.

I feel like shit ever saying that.

Friends and even non-friends call me "Moss," a truncated cop of my last name Mossovitz. My people embrace self-deprecating humor like a weapon, so I embrace the handle.

Almost nobody uses my first name, Ben. Only my parents—and it's during the required element occasions we break out the Torah—refer to me by my religious name, Benesh. In Hebrew, it means "blessed."

I suppose so, but there's a derogatory word which sets me off, and it rhymes with bike.

For a town which keeps its racism tucked inside soundproofed basements and far-flung barns outside the town limits, there's only one son of a bitch in Laytonville who's ever dropped that xenophobic tag on me.

Around town, people called Dave Kleban "Adolf" behind his back. I was the first and only guy to do it to his face. He'd neutralized me with the slur I hate so much and then spat on my shoes. The Aryan wannabe prick loved Red Man chew, so you can imagine my anger at being gobbed with brown chaw across my Addias ZX 5000. I may be punk, but I have *some* style.

For my retaliation, Adolf left me unconscious on the ground in the Laytonville High parking lot. I want to cry when I think of Greg bringing me back to with, of all things, a sour-smelling baloney sandwich he'd skipped for lunch.

What happened to Kleban at The Black Tarot, I'm not sorry about. I'm heartbroken for the horror which took the other guys at the show: Greg, Joey Ballard, Yancy Flueger, Nolan Julian, Hector Igartua, a few names of the 13 who were slaughtered within the first two songs of Dirty Trace's set.

One of the punks who'd left the gig early, Jimmy Marcinko, later said to me in the halls at school, "Man, that's beat what happened to those kids."

"That's beat," in our vernacular translating to something that mega-sucked. Also, a gross undersell in this case.

I can see Adolf's clean shaved dome glistening like burning hatred under the raised house lights at The Black Tarot. As if the rag safety-pinned to the top of his black leather jacket with the screaming emblem "HITLER YOUTH" wasn't venomous enough. A back patch for white power hucksters Skrewdriver covered the remainder of Dave's back. The front of his New Reich ensemble displayed a score of buttons toting far-right extremist bands Kolovrat, Skullhead, No Remorse, Landser and Stahlgewitter.

Dave prowled the floor of the club amidst the set change following the second band on the bill, a local skate core trio clad in identical aqua and white colored Airwalk Prototype canvas shoes calling themselves Strait Trax. They carried a marginal following of So-Cal wannabe skaters who could be picked out by the logos for The Circle Jerks, Agent Orange or *Thrasher* magazine plastered across their slight chests.

Said skateboard demographic gave wide berth to Adolf's hostile circumventions and random jerks of his middle finger to anyone looking at him longer than a few seconds.

It was no irony, when the club overhead tossed Dave, as a lone wolf skinhead already knocking kids flat to the floor in the slam pit, a snarky love letter with the brackish protest anthem from The Dead Kennedys, "Nazi Punks Fuck Off."

I say this, because that was my doing. I'm friends with the club's assistant manager, Isaac Hoffman, another dreidel spinner like me, only he keeps his yarmulke in place and hosts Shabbat every Friday night, despite his claim the orthodox are way too literal to the scriptures.

"No, fuck *you!*" I remember Dave bellowing like a bear through his angry, flushed cheeks. He threw his middle finger toward the P.A. speakers, then at the rest of us, despite our giving him his space.

During the Strait Trax set, Adolf had it out for Billy Paquette, the only punk-wrestler hybrid Laytonville High boasted. I saw the 7 Seconds logo upon Billy's thick torso lift and fall at least three times, as Dave pummeled him with forechecks more geared for the ice in Canada's brutal Iron League.

When I stop and think about it, I suppose I should share part of the blame for what happened that night. I'd poked the bear, and Adolf rose to the occasion once the third band played: Macho Nachos, the dumbest name for an experimental punk band trying to be the next Minutemen.

Dave decked everyone in sight during two songs of Macho Nachos' half hour set, since their shuck and ska vibe had little to do with moshing. Our resident Rude Boy, Todd Knight, was in his element, skanking with his fingers grasping at nothing on the floor—picking up sticks, the weird bop was called. It would've gone out of favor by now if everyone didn't like Fishbone so much.

Macho Nachos' lack of velocity only made Dave angrier, and it was then when I saw him slam his fists against the stage, drawing a stern warning from both Black Tarot bouncers who could've made him the meat of a man-schnitzel sandwich.

Something awful was going down.

"Eat my ass, motherfuckers!" Dave shouted, pulling away from the stage and simpering beneath the diagonal-positioned floor amp on stage left. Fast they were not, but Macho Nachos were loud and there was steaming mad skinhead Dave Kleban, the pulsing speakers pounding his sweaty, bald head and ears sticking out nearly as nerdy as Alfred E. Neuman's.

The longer Adolf hung there, the easier everyone else began to feel.

Not me.

Because I saw it.

I don't expect you to believe this part of the story, and frankly, it's better off if you don't. For me, and for those who died and received justice, artificial as it was.

You ever see those old movies, especially the black and white noir flicks where the shadows seem to jump all around each corner in nearly every frame? The actors being obtuse to it all, of course.

That's what I saw hovering around Adolf. A dark, traceable shadow growing feet above Dave, behind his back. Like those actors in their overdone pasty makeup to stand out in monochrome, he was oblivious to it.

I know what I know, because I saw this—whatever you want to call it. I call it a force of some sort. A force as black as the venue's name.

A force of evil.

It loomed over Adolf, then it appeared to pounce on him.

It happened, because the very next second, I saw Dave Kleban, who needed no further provocation, ignite like a berserker. His eyes went wide, furious.

Possessed.

I can't tell you the name of Macho Nachos' fastest song, a click shy of your standard Descendents or Bad Religion whirlpool starter. It doesn't even matter at this point.

All that matters is I stood outside the pit as guys began pumping their legs into a filed circle spin. They followed each other in tandem, hands touching shoulders for spacing purposes, before the inevitable breakaway and crashing of bodies ensued. Your standard slam. Guys who knew each other, hung out together, played this music in their bedrooms like it was private gospel. Guys who knew the unspoken rules.

Kerry Murphy took a spill of his own accord, and I was there to help him to his feet before Billy Paquette could.

I gave Kerry a gentle push back into the pit before I was tackled myself by a row of guys.

"Yyyyyyyeaaaaahhhhh!!!"

Adolf stood in place, pumping his fists, both covered with silver rings, one yielding the insignia of the German Luftwaffe. He'd come at everyone with a full charge, and he'd taken out seven guys at once. Kerry had gotten away, and he ran straight for the men's room.

"Pussy!" Dave blasted behind him.

Macho Nachos cut their pit mover short, and the lead singer/bassist said thank you before turning off his mike.

"Dick!" We all heard him shout at Dave, who was immediately cut off by the bouncers.

We only knew the bouncers by their first names, Larry and Paul. Almost nobody knows their last names, but they're Laytonville legends who carry the tag-team moniker "The Hit Squad."

The Hit Squad said not a word. Their massive biceps outclassed Dave's. If Larry and Paul were 'roiders, no one cared. That very second, The Hit Squad were goddamn heroes, even if their act of valor was ultimately inconsequential.

"The fuck off me!" Dave shrieked. Yeah, he actually shrieked, since I don't think he still had whatever had seeped into him at the time.

The Hit Squad hoisted Dave Kleban beneath his thick armpits and dragged him off the floor.

Man, if anything went right that terrible evening, it was Adolf's roughhoused ejection.

We cheered and whistled as Dave's steel shank combat boots thrashed and kicked all over the floor trying to get traction, to no avail.

"Sieg Heil, asshole!" Billy Paquette roared, throwing his right arm up and out in the customary Nazi salute.

We all took cue, punks and metalheads as a united front. We all swung our arms upwards and extended our hands in derision at Dave Kleban. Even the Macho Nachos guys . Dumb band name, but they have my eternal respect.

"Sieg Heil!" we mocked Adolf before he was jerked forcefully to the front door and bulldozed out by Larry. The real Hitler would've found the entire exhibition dishonorable.

The skate rats who'd come to the all-ages show to support Strait Trax were already gone, scrubbing the black "X" marks drawn across the tops of their hands down the sides of their clammy shorts instead of using sink water. "X" in a punk show denoting you're not of legal age to drink.

The tension simmered inside the club and the floor thinned out between the handfuls who could order at the bar and those who bragged (lied, mostly) they were sneaking beers and hits of whiskey behind their parents' backs.

We sent The Hit Squad another cheer as they lumbered past. They accepted our adoration with fleeting waves before taking their positions on each side of the stage. Killing Joke's "Fire Dances" was playing. I remember that for some reason.

"Man, kind of a weak turnout tonight," Kerry Murphy said after returning to the floor. He flipped his sweat soaked, straw-colored strands with a snap of his neck. He was one of the metalheads I genuinely liked. I'd turned him on to hardcore legends Black Flag. He'd turned me on to doom metal savants, Saint Vitus. I subsequently turned other punkers on to Vitus by taping and spreading around a copy of *Born Too Late*.

"The scene's dying, dudes," Greg said with a locked-in point I couldn't accept at face-value, but he was my friend and seldom wrong when issuing an opinion with conviction. Here, he was right. The only mohawk to be found in the joint was on Levi Brunner, and his was not the Liberty spike variety; Levi's was flattened and cropped close to his dome, like those old Screaming Eagles of the 101st Airborne.

"Metal's going down the shitter, too," Kerry offered by way of empathy, I suppose. More like a concentrated effort to fortify our new bonds. I laugh to think it wasn't too long ago when punks and headbangers were slagging each other. "Thrash, death and doom's all I care about since all the other bands are wimping out with that synthesizer shit. Fucking douche crews."

"Truth," I said.

"Hey, Moss," Greg leaned in to address me as Nuclear Assault's "Justice" rumbled throughout the club. Thrash, not punk, but a fitting number I knew was Isaac's doing. The Dirty Trace guys had quietly wormed onto the stage and were tightening drumheads, fidgeting with the mike stands and tuning up. "Does something feel weird to you tonight? I mean, other than the low turnout and Adolf losing his shit more than usual."

I wanted to tell Greg what I'd seen hovering behind Dave Kleban, but I suddenly doubted myself.

"I reckon not," I fibbed to my buddy, a guy I shared not only my music and Reese's cups with, but also my *Hustler* collection, which I'd successfully shoplifted eight months in a row.

"Yo, Moss," one of the other metalheads I was casual with, Devon Van Fleet, said approaching me. The dude was the only headbanger at school with a honey, the highly desirable junior, Kim Fiorito. An unfathomable match: a preppie and a grit. He was wearing a Queensryche shirt, I recall that much, but I never heard what Devon said.

I don't know how no one else saw it, but surrounding Devon was that same blackened cloud, emission, whatever you want to call it. It gaped like a charred mouth, swooping in on Devon, coal-colored extensions appearing to chomp down and swallow him.

The other guys were giving Dirty Trace the business with their sourpuss singing of the Cro Mags, but my attention shifted to Devon. He stopped nattering and I caught him squeezing his eyes shut in pain. As if he'd lingered upon the sun for too long.

It didn't take Dirty Trace long to be in position as Sam Kimbrough, the club's soundboard operator, flashed them a thumbs-up and they were tearing into a super-fast number announced by lead singer, John Elstad, as "You're a Statistic."

Greg tugged me into the mosh pit which was smaller than it was two bands ago, but everyone was suddenly batshit crazy from the momentum Dirty Trace was laying down.

Round and round we went, less concerned with bouncing off each other and more into the tribal element of slam dancing. We raised our feet high and stomped back down in ovular processions. It was fucking glorious.

Until Devon Van Fleet did the unthinkable.

Nobody had seen him slip away and hoist himself upon the edge of the stage. He'd been too fast for Larry, who was already aiming to pull him down, since the club has a no stage diving policy. John Elstad loved it, though, and he clapped Devon upon the back in mid-leap.

We punkers liked Devon in a general sense. His own tribe liked to call him a sellout behind his back, but you figure it was jealousy since they weren't pulling any sex action themselves.

This night, however, Devon Van Fleet became a monster.

Before everyone else did.

Nobody made a human catch-all for Devon. We were into our own moshing ecstasy, though I saw Devon in flight, and I gasped to see him pinpointing the necks of Yancy Flueger and Nolan Julian with outstretched arms.

The three of them toppled to the floor as Devon not only clotheslined his targets; he dazed himself once his forehead struck the floor. Devon didn't even feel it when his splayed hands got stepped on twice.

Dirty Trace had already slipped into their second (and last) song of the set, "Fear is Thy Name," as the pit halted, and everyone bent down to help Yancy and Nolan. Rude Boy Todd knelt to check on Devon, and that's when the shit really hit the fan.

The dark, malignant mass burst over the entire pit, as if feeding off the raised energy jacking up the fever to an unprecedented level of violence. Nobody else caught it.

Why was *I* the only dude who could see it? I backed as far away as I could get.

Within arm's reach of the bar, I watched hell explode in front of me. Like Devon and Adolf before him, every one of those guys on the floor turned into rabid dogs.

The music ground on and John Elstad was writhing and thrashing with the mike in his own lunatic fashion, his back to the crowd. The lighting was dim, and his band was playing too fast to see what was happening below.

Yancy knocked Todd out of the way with an upraised knee before screaming and bringing his foot down upon the shaggy head of Devon Van Fleet, who'd bit into his ankle. Yancy did it again and again until blood oozed all over the floor. A lulling of Devon's mashed face exposed his pulpy death.

I never took Laytonville High wrestler Billy Paquette as a thug, much less a punker, but unexpectedly he had a switchblade out and he didn't hesitate to ram it into the back of Yancy's neck. Billy was in such a fervor, he jerked the blade free as Yancy's blood spurted all over his face, then he began shivving Yancy in the lungs. Over and over.

As Yancy coughed up blood, Todd was back in action and if he looked goofy doing his skank routine, he was even zanier windmilling his way back to Yancy, catching a ralph of gore in his face. *Evil Dead* raids a punk show.

It didn't stop Todd as he swung for all his might. He missed Yancy, instead hitting Billy's arm, the blow enough to send the switchblade twirling out of any of their reaches.

In response, Billy punched Todd in the throat as Yancy collapsed to the floor. Todd had no time to gag, much less anything as Billy seized his head inside a brawny arm flexing out of his 7 Seconds shirt. I love that band, but they're forever tainted for me, thanks to Billy snapping Todd's neck with brawn I never fathomed him using to lethal effect.

"Somebody needs to call 911 now!"

That came from Larry, who took it upon himself to enter the fray, only to get clocked by none other than my good friend.

Greg seized Dirty Trace's guitar station mike stand (wires and all) and jousted Larry across the jaw with the base.

I haven't mentioned Jerry Haverhill and Wade Sparks to this point, but I will now. They were punkers from two counties away we routinely saw at shows. They gang hauled Billy Paquette to the floor and Wade drove his thumbs into Billy's eye sockets. Jerry flailed Billy's right side, working his ribs with cheap shot after cheap shot. In time, Billy was gone, his final scream courtesy of Wade returning his switch—into his skull.

"Screw the instruments!" I heard Dirty Trace guitarist Lee Swain shout as he dropped his slate Mosrite Venture Model II, the same model and color Johnny Ramone used. Still plugged in to his amp as he bolted backstage with the rest of the band, leaving a cacophony of distortion which covered the re-emergence of Dave Kleban.

Adolf had snuck back into the club, and I saw his eyes bug at the blood orgy The Black Tarot had turned in to.

"You think that 'Sieg Heil' shit was funny, Mossovitz?" Adolf hollered, pinpointing me away from the battle, as Greg mashed the mike stand into Jerry Haverhill's guts, then his nose. Haverhill dropped to the floor with my buddy pounding the shit out of him with that mike stand. I get the chills thinking about the moist clanging noises jockeying against the shrill feedback.

I had thus far been immune to the sable enigma turning everyone into savages, but all it took was Dave Kleban hitting me with that word. *That* word. Rhymes with hike and trike, and I'll be damned if I let anyone ever drop it on me again.

Whether it was from the phantom annihilation force or just my internal combustion toward Dave, I swung for his face.

I connected, but it didn't stop him. Worse, my hand blasted in horrible pain through my fingers, into my wrist. Luckily, I'd only sprained it.

"Was that supposed to *hurt,* bagel boy?" Dave taunted me, driving his fist into my guts.

I hadn't noticed everyone on the floor was now dead, except for Greg. Sam Kimbrough had chased Dirty Trace's trails to the VIP lounge. Larry was kayoed. His Hitman-in-crime, Paul, had vanished. Presumably to call the cops.

I nearly puked right there from Dave's wallop into my abdomen, and I cringed to see him raise his arms over his head, clenching his fists together.

He was about to lower the boom when I was tackled from the side by Isaac Hoffman. It hurt worse than my ineffective punch and my pummeled stomach, but Isaac had saved my life.

"Die, Nazi scumbag!"

I'm going to cry right now, if you'll excuse me. Those were Greg's last words.

I saw that horrid blackness not only submerge Dave but siphon into him, turning his eyes equally dusky. Murk belched from his exclamation of pain and laughter.

I wanted him gone. Forever.

It was Greg who died instead as Dave turned from me and Issac and with his fists still clenched, he swung like a batter chasing a high curveball and connecting.

Greg's expression of terror was forever locked as his head inexplicably separated from Dave's swing, rolling across the floor where we'd moshed all night. It rolled sickeningly, leaving a trail of smeary blood marks in its wake until bouncing off Kerry Murphy's lifeless hip.

"No!" I shrieked from my crumpled position on the floor. "I'll fucking kill you, Kleban!"

"Shut up, Moss!" Isaac pleaded as he attempted to shield me from what would've surely been our living end had Dave gotten his hands on us.

Gunfire echoed around the room and Dave Kleban dropped in front of us.

"Die, already," I seethed at him, but no such luck.

"F-fuck you, Mossovitz," Adolf growled at me. The bullet which tagged him had plunked him through his right shoulder, exiting cleanly through the pectoral. For his sharpshooting, Deputy Darren Taggert became an instant Laytonville celebrity.

Issac and I were interrogated for more than an hour, along with the bartenders, Larry, Paul, Sam and the members of Dirty Trace. To the beat reporter for *The Laytonville Times,* Jolene Byrne, a skinny redhead on her first post-college job, I finger-pointed Dave Kleban as the culprit, not to one murder.

All of them.

This after spinning the same story for the cops.

"Burn in S.S. hell," I growled at Adolf once the cuffs were slapped.

Isaac backed my recount, partly out of solidarity. Mostly because what had happened was so fucked up nobody would believe either of us. He won't confirm if he'd seen the black mass as I did. I don't blame him. Wherever it went to, I'm afraid to know.

It's been a few months since The Black Tarot Massacre, as has become known around the entire state. People talk about it as if they were there. Posers.

I'm doing my first Shabbat this Friday in years at Isaac's place. Za'atar fried chicken with spicy honey thyme, zucchini kugel for the appetizer. Kosher wine, reciting the Kiddush.

Issac and I will sing to honor friends gone and for the hopeful end of bigotry.

Wolf Con

Times have been tough for seasoned actors in the horror industry. All anyone wants nowadays are killer clowns turning people into pillars of gore, left wing driven eco-horror, demonic A.I., undead anything. Remakes of Stephen King adaptations, you can get greenlit hand-over-fist. Hell, even the vampires are getting a resurgence, the fluky bastards.

My last name isn't Cage, alas, thus I've had ongoing trouble as a decades long professional actor landing a role. Not even a bit part cameo in some Berkeley film school nerd's term project.

I've starred in 23 films, all werewolf themed. I've won two Saturn Awards in their horror bracket. People call me typecast, and I own it. I'm bloody *proud* of it. Nobody, save for my late husband, Robert, knows the reason I'm so convincing in my roles is because I'm the real deal, praise the Egyptian jackal god, Wepwawet.

You'd never know I'm old by the endurant Ovaltine malted streak through a full wave I'm crowned with when I should be whiter than that old goose narrating the last *Titanic* film. To be honest, I should be long dead by mortal years' count.

I used to have my hair coddled every few weeks by Sally Hershberger herself from 1967 to 1972. I was doing everything from American International to Hammer to Amicus films and could afford her then. Nobody fathomed, especially Sally, I was already carrying 76 years. 76 and fabulous, hiding a mad crush on Cary Grant, who was swinging both ways in his prime.

That was 56 years ago already. Time flies, even for the undead, when you're hungry for a handout.

Things have been so bad I nearly skipped paying my SAG membership dues this year. Only the family fortune Robert left me with has afforded me comfort, if not a stable career. I'd love to whip up a sunset ride with Nicholson in *Wolf 2*, since we'd knocked the idea around years ago in a Burbank hotel bar. There the proposal had been laid to waste with the hotel itself.

Thus, you can imagine the joy I felt being invited out to Colorado Springs for the first annual Wolf Con.

Yes, you've read that right.

Wolf Con.

I've seen weirdness on the convention circuit, and not just those Otakon girls who surgically alter their pupils to such horrifying lengths they make themselves living anime chicks. I know, you straight guys are already tumbling the Japanese phrase "bukkake" around in your sordid minds.

BronyCon, Dead Guy Days, Merfest, Anthrocon. Fetish Con, for you bukkake sickos.

I wish they'd had such a thing as Wolf Con when I was getting major parts twice a year from the Sixties through the center of the Big Eighties, before the glut of those *Friday the 13th* and *Nightmare on Elm Street* butcher bonanzas chased us loup-garou underground.

If you can imagine wall-to-wall cellulite packed inside horror geek chic, assless jeans and irresponsible spandex meandering around a convention center and caterwauling wannabe lycanthrope code to one another, then you have Wolf Con.

Some of the attendees are expert cosplayers prowling about in shredded flannel shirts with faux blood on their all-too-real bone-colored claws. The poor boy pretenders parade in silly rubber wolf masks from Spirit Halloween atop their street clothes. Almost all yield a werewolf flick splashed upon unanimously black tee shirts for *Wolfen, The Howling, Curse of the Werewolf, Dog Soldiers, She-Wolf of London* and *Brotherhood of the Wolf.*

I've even seen a handful of shirts splashed by the cover of Ozzy Osbourne's *Bark at the Moon.* The music's always been a bit too rowdy for my tastes, but the album came out in 1983, the same year I did *Bad Omens.* Bird-in-Hand, both became top draws of '83.

The heaviest go-getter tee delights me as an old schooler who was there to see its premiere firsthand at The Rialto in Akron, Ohio circa 1941. One year shy of my fifties. I'm talking Lon Chaney, Jr.'s signature *Wolf Man,* of course. The holy grail of the genre.

There's even a handful of people wearing shirts of other werewolf films I starred in: *Blood Cycle, Were-Warriors, Night of the Ahroun* and *Ragabash.* The latter atrocity being a cringeworthy eight scene appearance (just above a cameo) when I needed rent money. Long before there was a Robert in my life.

You can smell the sheath of body funk amidst the prevailing clog of greasy burgers and fries from the husband-and-wife vendors on the other end of the hall operating under the unfortunate name, Baron Von Wolfenstein. Many of the Wolf Con folks are chomping away on those slimy looking slabs inside red and white crisscross patterned paper boats as they sidle in close quarters from table to table.

The collective chatter ricocheting around Colorado Springs Convention Center is enough to pierce my waning hearing, but the next person who peels off an "ARROOOOO!" in my proximity is going to know a *real* werewolf's wrath. It's my vow, not a mere promise.

Sybil Danning is the keynote speaker of this wacky shindig celebrating lusus naturae. Nearly 80 years old, Sybil is still a hetero guy's wet dream. Her legendary tit pop scene in 1986's *Howling II: Your Sister's a Werewolf* (absolute rubbish of a film) is a common topic I hear passed between male slobs of all ages, one who confesses to enjoying a private crank to that passage across his cell phone.

We have Jason Bateman here at Wolf Con for his abysmal fortune to land the role Michael J. Fox no longer wanted in *Teen Wolf Too.* Sarah Patterson from *The Company of Wolves,* still an exquisite Red Riding Hood and drawing the most fan selfies aside from Emily Perkins and Katharine Isabelle, the Fitzgerald sisters from *Ginger Snaps.* Megan Follows from *Silver Bullet,* a movie I wish I could've shoehorned Everett McGill out of, is doing brisk business as well.

The vendor room of the Colorado Springs Convention Center is nearly as vast as The Royal Gorge about five miles away, and here is where my Meet and Greet table is relegated, away from the guests of honor set up in the main promenade. I'm just lucky the con committee spelled Wentworth Porpora correctly on page 11 inside the Wolf Con program. You'd be surprised how often I get called Wendell Poopora. It was funny the first time. More annoying with repeat offenses than that *Dances with Werewolves* twaddle.

"Pardon me, sir," I hear plenty loud, considering my hearing these days is starting to wane. The bulldog ralph is coming from a husky Hispanic man who's crammed himself into a one-size-too-small shirt for the werewolf western, *Blood Moon.* "Do you have any idea where the panel rooms are? I'm on one, speaking about the old *Werewolf by Night* Marvel comic."

"Afraid not, friend," I say with a shrug, as a line of people forms at my table, all at once.

Over the P.A., I barely hear traces of John Carpenter's spooky synth opening theme for *The Fog*. Not a werewolf film, of course, but still horror and still a hit with the conventioneers, which my laboring auditory capacities pick up their nattering "do-da-do-da-do-da-do-da-dooooos" in passing.

A mounted flat screen the size of a minor league outfield scoreboard across from my table is running *An American Werewolf in London* on silence. It boasts its own quailing audience right now, all these decades since its 1981 premiere. Rick Baker masterminding David Naughton's grotesque transformation is for my money, the only correct depiction of the noisome bone crunching, the agonizing extension of wrists and ankles, the protruding scales of the spine, the sprouting hair that sometimes feel like tiny razors. I can attest; the pain of it all feels like a goddamn heart attack thrashing the *outside* of your body.

My queue is now seven people deep, all peering around one another to make sure it's really me. This as some bumbling fatso clown wearing a *Star Trek* shirt to a horror con has the gall to slag me to his bumbling fatso girlfriend wearing the TARDIS time machine acronym from *Doctor Who*.

"Wentworth Porpora? Who the hell is that? The guy's got a lot of nerve charging so much for autographs and selfies as a fucking nobody."

I chomp down on that insult as much as I'd love to chomp down on the smug, plump prick and leave him, entrails hanging out under the lunar light of tonight's full moon.

Instead, I focus on my first visitor, a young woman who could be my great-great-granddaughter and her similar aged friend. They both sported the extra thirty dollars for the souvenir inaugural convention shirt, and both are pushing the Wolf Con logo to a severe stretch from their considerable chests.

"I wish you would have been in the *Twilight* series, Mr. Porpora," the first girl says to me with an endearing squeak. She has pencil thin legs stilting from a plaid skirt I find becoming paired with her auburn hair, pulled into a ponytail held in place by a matching scrunchy. By contrast, her friend is stuffed like a schmo into baggy denims, the apparent unisex norm of Colorado Springs. "You know, maybe in a quick cameo as a mentor to Jacob Black, or something. Make it out to Erin, please."

"It's my career that's fallen into twilight, I'm afraid," I tell her without unnecessary smarm. Much as I want to scream at Temple Hill Entertainment and Lionsgate for giving my *Twilight* audition reel the California no.

Erin is of a much younger age bracket, but she knows me as an actor, and her credit card clears my Square swipe for $60.00.

"May I come over to you so my friend can take the picture?" she asks with manners I find charming. Normally, I'm on guard against youngbloods zapping me from a distance for some TikTok roast set to an inglorious neo-hip hop track by mush mouthed rookie rappers bragging about their Glocks.

"Of course," I grant Erin, giving her an invitational gesture to swing around my table. Those waiting their turn show me their best smiles with similar designs for getting close to me.

If they could see me later tonight.

Erin wiggles her fists triumphantly to her friend, whom I hear called Anita, as I spot another pair of women, hands clasped with zero care for the random sneers shot at them. They're intent on gaining my attention.

The alpha of this couple, with her broad, squared shoulders, thick calves dumping from beneath a ratty pair of cargo shorts and a Basic Training buzz cut accented by a leprechaun tint, lifts the hand of her brunette partner, dainty by comparison. I can see they have matching black bands on the respective fourth fingers of their left hands.

The shapeless, tall alpha touts her trophy wife like I've seen too many times done by uber-possessive hetero males. They're both wearing Rainbow Coalition t-shirts, soggier on the near-anorexic brunette. Yet there's no mistaking their silent message to me through their gesture of raising their free hands with power-plying fists. They know who and what I am. Well, maybe not *all* of what I am. One thing about my coming out, it's greatly reduced the number of drunken bimbos asking me to Sharpie their cleavage.

I give the married ladies my most genteel nod and return a fist pump of solidarity. It's not missed by those standing in line. A few widen their pre-existing grins. Two could care less.

It's the incongruous beanpole dressed like this is Wall Street instead of Wolf Con who takes exception. His corporate accouterments gain more than a few awkward stares.

He slips out of line and snarls "Figures," at me, loud enough for everyone at my table to hear. Even above the whirling echo of horror geeks pointing at his maroon and navy-blue necktie like he's "The Man."

"Guess he didn't read my book," I say with a chuckle, nodding to the small stack of copies of *Under a Full Moon: The Autobiography of Wentworth Porpora* I have for sale at a reduced price of $22.00.

The ten-dollar markdown of my freak flag planting hurts far less than missing my late, beloved Robert. Yet I'm just as happy he's not here to witness such boorish behavior. Not that we were never used to prejudice as a couple when he was still alive. We'd tied the knot in a private ceremony, under a harvest moon before the climax of our mutual transformations. Our officiant, Stefan, was a werewolf, like us, the only witness before and after the ceremony.

"Could you act like you're about to eat me?" Erin requests, also loud enough to cut through the prevailing din. It's faint and my ears are ringing and cloudy, but I somehow hear some dork tell his companion, "Can't believe Sybil signed my glossy 'With love!' Sick!"

"Acting's about *all* he'll do," Joe Wall Street scowls from the open crease at the neckline of his sky blue Van Heusen. He could use a clean shave, given the bristly, hard swallow of his Adams apple. I want to see it severed and fountaining crimson.

"To my face," I jeer back at him, keeping my tongue in place from the delicious prospect of gobbling him gone. "I'll give you that much, sir. Your anti-gay rhetoric has more style than the prototype internet trolls. Nonetheless, crass is crass and a coward's a coward, behind a keyboard or in the flesh."

"Point to Wentworth Porpora," the next person waiting in line says with a welcome step forward closer to my table, blocking Joe Wall Street from encroaching my comfort zone. A spot that could cost his life.

"I used to think you were such a badass of your time, *sir,*" is Joe Wall Street's sarcastic retort before slinking away toward the convention hall doors. Where the time has gone so quickly is a mystery, since the jumbotron is full of garish glee as David Naughton ransacks Piccadilly Circus in his full wolf form. My innards seethe with delight and jealousy. Baker would've been out of a job had I landed that coveted role plotted in my motherland.

"Much appreciated," I say to my defender, who says nothing back, save for his beam of satisfaction at having done a good deed.

"Now where were we, Miss?" I get out after blowing a hard sigh through my nostrils. Hiding the momentary annoyance. I'm back in game mode, as if someone called for action.

"Erin," she offers her name again, splaying her hands outwards and tilting her head backwards, already in pose with a mock shriek. "And would you mind grabbing my ponytail like you're pulling my throat up to chew upon it? I'll pay extra if you want."

I've had stranger requests from fans in my lifetime. The guy in Detroit comes to mind who wanted me, after reading my book, to pose like he was giving me a knobber. Such debasing would've been cheating on Robert, though, even years after my dear spouse shot himself.

Using a silver bullet.

I oblige Erin, twisting her gingery hair into my fist, albeit gently. My free hand is clawed and purposefully positioned well away from her pillow-sized right breast.

Through her grey Wolf Con t-shirt, I see a newly emerged indentation jutting through the fabric where her substantial left breast is.

For Christ's sake, the young thing's turned on.

"Erin, honey, your headlights are on!" her friend teases with her cell phone pointed at us.

"I know, Anita, take the picture already!"

"I wouldn't post it on social, just saying!"

"My best friend is also another mother I don't need," Erin moans at me, staying in her mugged pose. Her bare nipple might as well be on public display at this point.

That's when I want this picture over as fast as possible.

"Thank you, Mr. Porpora," Erin says, giggling to Anita as I release her hair, and they quickly depart.

My interposing guest identifies himself as Charles as he whips out his VISA bank card with the same order as Erin.

I inhale and shake Charles' hand, grateful for the calming, callused sensation of another man before I'm compelled to look around him. I have no idea why, but I do.

I know what you are, Porpora, I hear a crackled female voice punch into my subconscious brain.

No mystery, even with her lips sealed shut. I spot an older woman with alluring platinum hair tumbled all around her shoulders which are encased in a black one piece showing off a figure a woman forty years her junior would kill to have.

That's not what mesmerizes me.

It's the glistening pentagram shining at her sternum which nearly has me telling Charles and everyone else waiting to come back in an hour.

You've enjoyed the scam of a lifetime, my friend, starring in werewolf films when you've been one yourself since the end of World War I. Come find me later, after these fools retire to their own idiocy. Come as you really are. Praise Selene and Tivaci, this will be a glorious moon.

The crone wolf, as I've deduced her to be, fires me a knowing wink before blending into a newly arrived crowd of coeds from the University of Colorado Boulder. They're wearing custom made jerseys advertising their soon-to-be alma mater and stitched patches calling their small band of five, "The Wolf Pack." They look ridiculous with their furry hoods sporting stupid dog ears, and shaggy gloves with plastic talons jutting from homemade slits at the fingertips.

"Can you do the same thing as the girl, Mr. Porpora, only go for my throat with both hands?" Charles asks with the first betrayal of his deep-inhabited dweebishness. *"Ragabash* rules, by the way."

Bag of shit is what I used to call that awful dreck to Robert, who agreed wholeheartedly, calling it the most desperate low of my career. Gordon Levitt was a hack director, but the tawdry schlock paid my living expenses for nearly a year.

"Indeed," I say to Charles graciously, remembering how long it's been since *Ragabash* came and went and I've had no role of substance since.

***

It doesn't take me long to find her, even in wolf form.

To the outside observer, the old woman's growl would indicate threat.

With her silver fox coat, and a snap of her snout upwards, I have no problem interpreting her guttural rumbling as a greeting of welcome.

The silhouette of the craggy Laramide Orogeny in the Garden of the Gods beneath the beam of the Blood Moon (rock formations boasting the most profound tint of red under sunlight) and the scattered constellations makes me want to bay at the beauty of it. A spectacular way to ring my 133rd birthday tomorrow.

"What the hell?" I hear to my right, now on all-fours, making me snap my fur-coated neck in the voice's direction. I feel an all-too-familiar sensation lighting up my gullet. The voice seems familiar, but that doesn't matter much, considering all the people who'd come to see me at my table today. Depending on how tomorrow goes at Wolf Con, I'll be heading home nearly a grand richer after my layouts for flight and hotel. Robert would've been so proud of me.

The figure slumped to the ground is but a barely discernible meat bag despite the gleam from the sky, but all I need know in this guise is the super thin frame of what appears to be a male human.

"How did I get here?" the man croaks groggily and I can only detect the folded collar of his button-down dress shirt, finger pointing him as if we were back in the convention center.

An early birthday gift for you, my new friend, I hear, though in this form, it sounds squelchy, like a nattering bug come to life, instead of from what I know to be an elder wolf. *He will not be missed, I assure you.*

Even with relative darkness, I see her eyes ignite a white phosphorus color. The movies would have you believe werewolf eyes are golden or plasma red. Not true, and never more apparent from the old werewolf, who peals into the night sky like she's having an orgasm.

I get a crystallizing vision of a third wolf amongst us and a Canis latrans beside him. The bloodlust gorges inside my throat, then my jowls. Somehow, I know who these ghosts are. Gods, actually. Tivaci, the great father wolf of people more ancient than I, plus his keen brother, Coyote. Normally in conversion, I seldom think with such lucidity, but I swear with certainty the Shoshone and Bannock god Esa once ruled these parts.

"Acting's about all *he'll do,"* I hear a phantom echo amidst the conjoined caterwauling between lycanthrope and sandstone divinities from the beyond, lending their chittering yowls of antediluvian lexicon. My course of action has been figured. Predestined, it would seem, given the magnanimity of indigenous lords forcing my hand.

I join my crepuscular voice to theirs, drool spilling between my hungry incisors, trickling down my canine cheeks into a pelt about to be drenched in blood.

I send Joe Wall Street to meet his own hateful maker after ripping his throat out.

Even as a werewolf, I know for certain I'm smiling. It feels nearly as opulent as my wedding day in 2001.

Tivaci nods at me, engulfed by a benevolent plume matching the azure pupils of my new friend who tears into Joe Wall Street's bowels. The bottom half of the necktie is sectioned off with them. All the pale skinned suit can do is gurgle with a sickening echo into the rocky spires of the garden's Three Graces.

***

I end my tenure at the first edition of Wolf Con reluctantly signing the boobs of some crackered up girl whose shit heel of a boyfriend puts her up to it. After getting Jason Bateman to mark up her mammary glands before me. I know I look unenthusiastic about it, but I can't speak of the real reason for my haggardness. I simply say thank you as the girl stifles down her bile and tries not to tip over her wine in a pathetic stagger.

My back is to the thin trickle of holders-on scouting for last minute discounts from vendors looking to lighten their loads for the trips home as I pack my books and glossy pics into my plastic carry tote. I'm tired from the prior night's festivities, thus I don't recognize the voice.

"See you next year, Wendell?"

I grunt and sigh before gnashing out, unable to control my pissy tone, "It's *Wentworth*."

"Gotcha, young man," I hear with a cackle that sounds even more lurid than the wolfish version. A whirl of black fabric swishes into periphery and I know her, just as I've become familiar with her scent, the same as both human and non. Tinged with Naked Bee coconut and honey hand repair cream.

"Young man?" I quip with relief, catching the sparkling pentagram dangling beneath an accumulation of neck wrinkles I didn't spot before. The old woman's still stunning to me, given how our snouts and teeth were down in the gore together. "You don't even want to know what age I am today, Crone."

"As long as you say 'Crone' with respect, I'll confess to you, *young man,* I was there to see the Confederates hit the bricks after the carnage in Gettysburg. Feasted on soldiers from both armies on Culp's Hill. Let *that* swim in your mind a moment, son."

"The hell you say?" I gasp, wanting to bow before her and I do just that. "How does one of our kind make it so long?"

"By knowing the difference between carbon and silvern, for one reason," she jokes, twiddling the pentagram talisman between fingers so gnarled yet advertising a hint of unimaginable strength. I saw those same fingers in werewolf form slinging Joe Wall Street's entrails before the spectral forms of Tivaci and Coyote as an offering. Reading my mind to scary effect, even for werewolves, she adds, "They were appeased, if that matters. Angelica is my name."

"About last night," I say, finding nothing of greater substance to offer.

"Do stay in touch," Angelica tells me with the same wink she fired me yesterday. "Last night was about easing some of your personal suffering. You may have noticed your hearing has sharpened since last night. Tivaci's reward to you. I hope from here on out, you can consider me a friend amongst these clueless twits."

I know I'm the only one who can see it as Angelica disappears into thin air, while I catch dejection from the book huckster across from my table, who's done poorly in sales all weekend. Even with a last-minute sale of *Under a Full Moon: The Autobiography of*

Wentworth Porpora, he looks shattered. Bless his kind soul, he's waving it at me, knowing he's snagging a sale that should be mine.

I give a nod of consent to my neighbor vendor, who now looks downright ashamed. As Angelica alluded, my hearing's far better than usual today, and with the dwindling foot traffic, he tells his customer to come see me for an autograph.

"Dude, I love *Ragabash!*" the guy shouts, whirling around to show off his shirt bearing the film's movie poster, far scarier than the film itself.

Ragabash may be a bag of shit, but this is the grandest 133rd I could've asked for.

The Cleansing of the Soles

The Givenchy sneakers clumped around the drier's rotating drum like the rumbling floor toms from Manic Augustinians drummer Shay McDaniels. A band no doubt reconsidering their lyrical huckstering of self-deprecation and suicide after tonight's meet and greet of death.

Sha-shunk-a-thunk. Repeat pattern.

I was missing Donna three months after her curt parting. Senselessly longing for her bickering over my accumulation mania. "Hoarding," she'd called it, always to set me off.

I seized those shoes the minute fate drove them my way amidst the adrenalized turmoil murder brings. Shucked and scattered somehow. An untagged forensics exhibit, all mine.

The blood was problematic.

The pricey kicks belonged to Manic Augustinians guitarist, Marc Roberson. Late as of five hours ago.

Listening to the groaning motor fan and repetitive banging of those shoes, I'm sitting cross-legged in front of the machine, relishing the hot air massage. It casts the first aura of triumph I've enjoyed since forever.

I'm fanning through a crate filled with handwritten set lists I've poached over the years. I got another one for the collection tonight, though I'd hoped for Roberson's autograph at the band's bus. Maybe a selfie.

Impossible to get either of those now, the rear parking lot then filled with the arresting canvas of shock dashed by twirling police cherries. The lookee-loos ushered away from Marc Roberson's shivved corpse. The cuffed and giggling culprit covered in crimson, claiming he did it as "the band's ultimate fan."

Hardly the first time I've plundered treasure from a dead rock god.

The Equine of Loch Raven

"I'm not sure I've had enough coffee for this yet," Detective David Amsler objected from behind the wheel of the Impala, poking at the in-car GPS system, setting the route directions for 2520 Elphin Drive with his forefinger.

"You've had enough," his partner, Christine McCann, jabbed playfully back at him. "In fact, Rina told me a week ago it's a good thing you're not an orthodox family for the diet you keep. Or lack thereof."

"Heh," Amsler chuckled back at her. "Just because we haven't observed Shabbos on a Friday in years, I get such treason."

"Between us girls, she also called you a goyim for putting Miracle Whip on a pastrami sandwich. Even I know better than that, Amsler. You're a bigger gentile than I am."

"Yeah, yeah, my grandmother would be turning over three times in her grave right now calling me a meshugener. Miss you, Bubbie."

"We're not stopping for a third round of coffee, just saying," McCann told him as an endpoint.

"You're a bigger ballbreaker than Rina."

"Good thing you married her instead of me, then."

"Tell me you don't believe this Baxter kid's story," Amsler said, changing the direction of the conversation. He tugged his burgundy paisley patterned necktie loose and unfastened the top button of his white Van Heusen dress shirt, feeling more than the fabric flump. The bulge at his neckline said his partner's harassment was merited.

"We'll see if her story stays consistent," McCann answered with a tentative sigh, flicking a tumble of her sandy wave off her brows with a hard flip toward her right. "Hard not to write the idea of a killer horse off as creative assembly."

"Bullshit, in other words," Amsler moaned. "Who in the world would buy such an absurd story, McCann? A magical monster-horse? Come on. I played a lot of Dungeons and Dragons in college, sure, but—"

"Which explains why you're a such a dork," McCann provoked him again.

"Can you be serious for a second?" Amsler snapped at her, his untrimmed eyebrows writhing. "We're talking about the mauling and drowning of a twelve-year-old boy, Mason Ridgely. His best friend, a girl of the same age, claims our perp is a horse that reportedly lives in the water. I feel as ridiculous as I sound."

"Your Bubbie would probably call us *both* meshugeners, then," McCann shot back with less comicality. "Because I was going to mention there's something like the girl's describing in Scotland. Some nutty water phenomena and I'm not talking about the Loch Ness Monster. I forget what it's called, but it'll hit me later. Look, I'm as dubious as you are. The only viable suspect is the same as the only viable witness. Another kid."

"Who'd have to be as strong as a professional wrestler to lay the kind of beatdown Mason Ridgely suffered. You can't tell me Hannah Baxter can out-bench Duane Johnson."

"Then who killed Mason Ridgely?"

***

"Take the AirPod out of your ear, honey," Lenora Baxter instructed her daughter. There was no muster to the mother's voice. No firmness. No authority. She sounded as slumped as her defeated posture and her mousy housewife's mop. No longer carrying the distinction of wife, the preliminary interview report had noted.

It was almost to be expected, then, when the chestnut-haired Hannah Baxter looked at her mother with indignance. This was no mere defiance; it was outright dismissal. Her rude candor made the cutesy emoji with hearts for eyes splashed across her pink t-shirt look contentious.

"This is important," Lenora said, again without conviction.

Neither detective needed to speak it to know what the other person was thinking. One look at Hannah's dug-in slouch upon the sofa and a crossing of both her arms and legs, the single AirPod still latched inside her left ear canal; it all clattered with immaturity. Even before Hannah uttered snottily, "I can hear them."

"I know you've already answered these questions before," Amsler said calmly, taking the lead.

"Then why do I have to answer them again?" Hannah returned with disturbing self-entitlement; her countenance was as cross as everything else on her. "This is stupid and so are you. Too stupid to believe me, so why bother?"

"Hannah Jane Baxter!" Lenora exclaimed, the sudden flush across her cheeks looking like immediate twin sunburns. No longer docile. Lenora was not only exasperated. All the frustration of her presumed domestic woes came raging forth in response to the embarrassing behavior of her bratty daughter.

"What?" Hannah sneered back. "I'm telling the truth! It happened the way I said it did!"

Lenora sprang from her easy chair next to the sofa and not even Hannah herself could've predicted how quickly her mother snagged the earpiece out, confiscating it along with the girl's Apple phone.

"Hey!" Hannah shouted, but this time there was fear instead of insolence.

"You will answer the detectives' questions, and you will do so with respect, young lady!"

"I didn't kill Mason!" Hannah screeched, unfurling herself and scrambling toward the edge of the sofa. Had she not stopped there, both detectives might assume the young girl was trying to make a break for it, like a felon at an arraignment hearing with lax bonds. "Mom, I didn't! I swear it!"

"Then tell the detectives the truth," Lenora said, bringing her voice down a notch. It was composed, though still carrying an edge. A tone reiterating her daughter would no longer dictate things.

"What more is there to say?!?" Hannah shrieked, despite. "Mason and I were walking down Merryman's Mill Trail, the one you and Mason's parents let us go down all the time."

Amsler shot McCann a look of recognition between them before asking, "You pick up the trailhead right down the road from here, is that correct, Hannah?"

"Yes," Hannah responded to Amsler with a brisk nod. "Me and Mason have done it countless times. It's always been safe. We bring snacks in Mason's bookbag, the one with all the Marvel superheroes on it. We go there and skip rocks, hang out."

"Did he bring the bookbag this time?" McCann queried, leaning closer toward Hannah.

"No, not this time," Hannah answered with a shrug. "I'm not sure why and I'm not trying to be a pain, but what does that have to do with anything?"

Lenora gave her daughter a nod of approval for the attitude adjustment.

"It might have had something we could've used to determine who killed your friend," Amsler said, realizing his knees were idling with anticipation and ordering a silent stoppage to their bouncing.

"You mean *what,*" Hannah countered, keeping an air of respect to her rebuttal. "It was a thing, not a person."

"How would you describe what you saw, Hannah?" McCann prompted, lifting all clouds of judgment. It was often hard to negotiate with children, much less get proper testimony without a dotted lie or two. McCann could tell Hannah was still terrified by her ordeal; her crass behavior earlier obviously being a defense mechanism.

"It started as a horse, golden colored with a fluffy white mane," Hannah said, blowing a puff through her lips as she collected her thoughts before resuming. "I told Mason not to touch the horse. It was cool, though, you know? I mean, who gets to see a horse up close like that without a rider?"

"That's just the thing, isn't it?" McCann asked, patting both of Hannah's hands with her own. Amsler watched with satisfaction, knowing where she was leading Hannah. "There was no rider."

"Exactly," Hannah answered, letting herself relax a bit more. "I told Mason to back away and let the horse go by, but the horse stopped. God, it was pretty. When it was still a horse."

"When was it not a horse?" McCann edged forth, putting out an easing motion with her hand to Lenora, who was beginning to look antsy again. McCann had gained the child's trust, and she was going to maximize her advantage without invoking a needless shakeup.

"After the horse took off down the trail with Mason on it. There wasn't even a saddle. I can't believe Mason was able to stay on there all that time."

"How did Mason climb on the horse, then?"

"I know this sounds, like, really dumb, but the horse bowed down with its front legs. Does that make sense?"

"Yes, it does," McCann said with assurance, clasping her hands together in front of Hannah. "My grandfather used to breed horses for show. So, I assume you gave chase?"

"As fast I could, anyway. I mean, who can outrun a horse without a car?"

"True," McCann chortled. "The horse then bucked your friend off near the water."

"Yeah," Hannah affirmed with a single up and down shake. "By the time I caught up to them at the reservoir, I could see the horse looking back, like it was waiting for me. Like it wanted to—"

Hannah paused as her face flushed and tears scoured her cheeks. Lenora covered the distance between them, latching around her daughter in such a blink one would've assumed she'd teleported there.

"It's okay, Hannah," McCann told her, patting the young girl's knee while her mother smothered her sobs. "We won't be much longer. I know how upsetting this must be."

"You know horses, then," Hannah blubbered, pushing away from her mother's considerable bosom.

"A good bit, yes," McCann replied. "I'm no expert, but I did my fair share of horseback riding on my grandfather's farm."

"Can a horse smile at you? I mean actually smile?"

"I think I know what it was you were trying to come up with on the ride over, McCann," Amsler interjected. "Something I'm remembering from an old mythology class. Hannah, what happened next? You saw the horse smile at you. It threw Mason off its back. Then what?"

"I don't care who believes me at this point," Hannah answered through her sobs. "That crazy horse *smiled,* like it was *making fun* of me, knowing I couldn't do anything to help Mason. Then the horse launched Mason into the air, and he landed on his head. I could see his neck twist. I heard it, too. I'll never forget that cracking sound. God, it was sickening. He was dead right away."

"What else happened to Mason?" Amsler quipped, taking heed of adding to the girl's stress. Mason Ridgely's autopsy report had yet to be finalized, but thus far, Chief Medical Examiner Chuck Newton had listed numerous contusions, broken vertebrae, fragments of bone piercing Mason's brain, shattered bones and ribs all around the boy's five-foot one frame. Nothing indicating the cause of death from drowning, though Mason's body had indeed been drenched.

"Just like I told everyone else before you, the horse stomped on him!" Hannah exclaimed. "I don't remember exactly how many times, but it was a whole bunch! I was screaming and I was scared, but nothing like when that horse got into the water and pulled Mason in with its teeth. The horse's teeth were yellow and bloody! Disgusting! I wish I was lying about this, I really do, but after getting Mason into the reservoir, the horse turned into water itself! You know, like that liquid Terminator guy that couldn't be killed?"

McCann shot Amsler a look they each confirmed with single nods. Amsler creaked his mouth and McCann heard him begin to say "Kel—" before clamming up.

"It turned into a water horse! I'm not talking about those dumb Hippocampi from Percy Jackson, either! It was all water in the shape of a horse! It had Mason out deep before the horse kinda fell apart and they sank together."

"I'm so sorry you had to go through this, Hannah," McCann said.

"Do you believe me?"

"Honey, I don't know if I—"

"Last question, Hannah, and we'll go," Amsler chimed in.

"Do *you* believe me?" she asked the same of him, wiping her soggy face down the sides of her shirt. Amsler thought of the tee's giddy emoji suddenly curdling into that silly emoticon with gushers erupting from its grief-stricken cartoon face.

"I believe you didn't kill Mason," Amsler told her back, making sure Lenora saw the same guarantee in his eyes. "The injuries he suffered are beyond your possible strength, no offense."

"None taken," Hannah said with a nervous chuckle shared by everyone in the living room.

"How did Mason get back onto the shore if he was already dead? Did you see how?"

"Yes, and I'll tell you only if you promise not to send me to the looney bin."

"Promise," Amsler confirmed with a smile he gave his own children, one speaking of dependability.

"A monster came out of the water. Hideous, like one of those gross *Walking Dead* zombies I'd been talking to Mason about before it all started. The monster had Mason's body in its hands, and it told me I'd be next if I ever came back."

***

"Kelpie," was the first word spilling from Amsler's mouth once the Baxter house was out of view from all mirrors on the Impala.

"Hard to believe they exist even in Scotland," McCann said, feeling half foolish. "My grandfather used to tell me about kelpies when I was a little girl, and he'd have me help feed the horses. He claimed to have seen one in a loch on a trip to Falkirk in his own youth. He said it was a fast-moving body of water skimming across the plane in the shape of a horse. That's all he had to say. I thought it was a neat story, but I didn't believe him."

"Let's get nuts for a moment," Amsler said back, tossing McCann a pair of googly wide eyes for emphasis. "I'm willing to entertain the idea in the privacy of this car that everything Hannah said is true. *She* sure believes it. So, if this is really a kelpie we're dealing with and kelpies are supposed to be native to Scottish lochs, how did one get over here to Maryland, much less the United States at all?"

"You think I know?" McCann fired back, trying to keep her voice from rising. "You and I have seen some wild shit over the years. Laced-out drug addicts swallowing blood-soaked band aids, sadistic teenagers shoving foreign objects up the rectums of cats, prostitutes turning tricks in full display on the side of a bridge. None of that compares to what we've just heard. The only thing that makes sense the location of the crime."

"Loch Raven," Amsler finished for her. "It's a consistency, at least."

"But an actual living water horse monster? Where were the hoof prints? Divots, at least, something backing up the claim of an actual horse? Forensics found nothing, Amsler! If it was galloping as fast as Baxter said, it was sure to have left its mark somehow. Coming back to reality, if it was a human who'd done the dirty work, there were still no reported signs of a struggle at the scene. No imprints, save for where it was assumed Mason Ridgely fell to his death. Other than Mason's body, not a clue of anything."

"In the off-chance Hannah is covering something up—"

"No, Amsler, I agree with you. That girl believes what she saw."

"This'll be a hell of a report."

"You're the writer of the team," McCann said with a hint of envy. "But I think we should double back and have another look at the crime scene first."

***

McCann and Amsler scanned the perimeter of Loch Raven Reservoir, quiet for a Sunday with only a few sweaty weekend hikers and one detectable schooner drifting on the horizon with two likewise quiet fishermen. One of them gave McCann a distant wave, which she returned, rumbling to herself for not only having to work on a Sunday but at the grinding absence of resolution to this case.

Amsler seemed to be relishing it. Eyes widened, a compulsive licking of his upper lip, an excitable pacing and crouching around the warbling bank. He hadn't shaved since it had been a scheduled day off and there was growing oiliness to the recession at his hairline. A teenager on graduation day couldn't look more pleased with himself than Amsler right now.

Telltale signs he was on to something.

"The last time I saw you this wound-up, it was the Jefferson Mitchell bust."

"Getting that butcher narcotrafficker out of Greenmount East and into Baltimore City Detention's one of the greatest moments of my career. Even sweeter it was one of his fences who'd fingered him. Rina and I polished an entire bottle of Shiraz in celebration. Find me a stick, will you, McCann? A small one. Pencil-sized."

"You find something in there?"

"I'm thinking. Not water moss nor the breakoff from a siphonophore. It's stringy but the color doesn't match either of those. What breed of horse did Hannah claim it was?"

"She didn't," McCann answered him, scooching at a slouch a few paces away from the water until she found a crooked but sturdy twig cast along the gritty trail. As if lying in wait precisely for this moment of need. "But that description has me thinking of a Palamino. Here you go. Longer than a pencil, but I think this should do."

"Thanks," Amsler said, nudging the stick into the water.

"I'm not saying I wholly buy the kelpie thing," McCann said as her partner angled the stick inside the drink. He was meticulous in his business and not having immediate luck, she detected with a furrowed curiosity he never saw. "What I do know is Hannah Baxter didn't do it. She *couldn't* have. Mason Ridgely was murdered, though, can we agree?"

"A hundred percent," Amsler responded, poking into the rippling plane, which pushed back toward them both with faint gurgles.

"The question is who did it, and I can tell you it's nagging me so much the only way I'm getting any sleep tonight is to pop two melatonin."

"Okay, so we know Merryman's Mill Trail is popular with the locals," Amsler replied, matter-of-factly, stirring the stick inside the water like he was making soup right on the bank. Whatever he was after was more persistent than him by avoiding its extraction. "Though it's been sparse today, which I'll chalk up to the Orioles being at home this weekend, a playoff berth on the line. A buddy of mine had an extra ticket for me. Instead—"

"Tell me you've seen some indicative hoof prints, any extracted clods, anything which appears excessively pressed down to the ground. Anything to back up the claim of a horse having come through, because I sure as hell don't. Don't tell me it's one of your hunches, either, Amsler. I call those cop outs."

"Rina used to say the same thing whenever I'd come up with any excuse to avoid Sukkot after Yom Kippur. Seven days. Build and decorate the sukkah, collect the willow branches, recite the Hoshanot at synagogue, yadda yadda. King Jeroboam never had the lifestyle of a homicide investigator in mind all those centuries ago."

"Getting back to our wackadoodle kelpie or no kelpie case," McCann harrumphed at him.

"Alright, McCann," Amsler retorted, nowhere near as put out as he sounded, lancing what he was after with the stick, pulling it up and out carefully. "I don't know if kelpies really exist, but I'm going to need a baggie for this. It either washed up recently, or Forensics missed it entirely, but if this isn't golden hair, I don't know what it is."

"Son of a gun," McCann whispered as she moved in closer, already pulling out a plastic evidence bag from the right pocket of her navy-blue Nike windbreaker. "My grandfather would be the last word if he was alive, but I'd bet your next paycheck that is indeed horsehair."

"Nice," Amsler tittered as he gently shook the thin fibers into the baggie, which McCann sealed on instant before holding it up toward the sky.

"Doesn't validate anything other than a horse being in the area," McCann told him.

"I'm not much of an outdoorsy guy," Amsler said to her, rising to stand with twin pops cracking off from his knees. No expected mockery from his partner came. "Loch Raven Reservoir has what, 20 different trails? 22, I think? Plenty for horseback riding aside from hikers."

"What's your point?" McCann quipped, feeling a bang between her temples announcing a forthcoming headache. "Other than there really was a horse and—"

"It was being ridden already, and not by Mason Ridgely."

"You think someone on horseback is our actual killer?   Someone Hannah Baxter may know and is too scared to rat out?"

"She'd be a hell of an actress," Amsler answered, continuing to scout the water. "It's a scenario as preposterous as this entire case, but it makes a lot more sense than a demonic horse."

As if to scorn Amsler, the water sluiced instead of babbled.

If a water body of relative stillness such as a loch could elevate and roll like a hard, fat wave at high tide, and moreover, heading for Amsler and McCann, it was incredibly doing so right now.

"Holy shit!" Amsler exclaimed, feeling a twinge fire through his lower back as he twisted awkwardly to face what was forming behind him.

"That's impossible," McCann added to the startling expansion.

Instead of crashing at the bank, however, the massing water stayed in one place while morphing into shape. To see a formless element mold into a living, aquatic being wasn't merely abnormal. It wasn't even magical. This was pure grotesquery as it shaped a steed's head, a mane of streaming water flinging droplets through the air across its clear, globular back.

Emerging into a fluid, loch borne horse.

The left front leg rose and fell back down three times, making frightful splashes from where its hoof would be. Even in its translucent marine form, the horse looked angry as hell.

"Amsler, get away from there!" McCann shrieked as the watery horse tramped its way ashore, immediately assuming the tangible form of a *real* horse.

Its gilded coat beamed of munificence caught beneath the sunlight. The frilly white mane, soft by emergence. As scary as the prospect of it was, there was something compelling to the horse creature's inviting textures.

There was no saddle, no bridle. As the otherworldly horse raised the opposite front hoof, free of an iron shoe, and planted it back down upon the edge of the bank, the pounding sounded meaty.

The schooner McCann had waved to earlier was nowhere to be seen. No boats of any kind. She flash-checked the ascending trail over her shoulder, praying someone who could've cared less about the baseball game against the Texas Rangers had come straggling down.

No such luck.

"It can't be," McCann whispered, reaching inside of her windbreaker for her shoulder holster, which held her loaded Smith & Wesson M&P 9. Her body felt heavier than usual to move, as if she'd been weighed down with one of those twenty-pound vests plugged with sandbags extreme sport enthusiasts trained in. "*You* can't be."

Yet the Palomino horse staring down McCann, turning momentarily from Amsler, bobbed its head up and down and snorted, as if to say, *Lady, I'm not only real, you're going to wish you never got on to me.*

Terrifying enough, but the real kicker was the sudden ignition of reddish-orange flares filling both eye sockets of the Palamino, making McCann gasp as she fumbled for the handle of her gun, not yet jerking it free.

Amsler was faster to react.

His Glock 22 was already out and pointed at the horse, which whinnied shrilly at him. It screeched like a banshee, turning those firebrand eyes from an unspoken Hell upon him with full intent of stopping him cold.

It bore a set of gore-dashed teeth as the water spawned Palomino chomped down on Amsler's southpaw firing hand. He'd managed to squeeze off a round as the shot echoed around them, followed by

Amsler's bellow of agony before his Glock toppled from his grasp, landing at the tide.

"Amsler!" McCann screeched, finally getting herself together to whip out her pistol as she saw her partner inexplicably lifted from his feet by the horse's ferocious gnaw upon him.

Still roaring in shock, Amsler was whipped away from the water's edge by the horse, slung to a brief, deceiving abandon. Bleeding all over the ground from the bite which had snagged a nasty chunk out of his left wrist, Amsler couldn't say anything else as the leviathan in Palamino form arched backwards, powering itself on its rear legs, the musculature rippling as it lifted its front hooves up high.

The repulsive sound of Amsler's head being pulped by the slamming of those hooves not once but twice made McCann want to vomit, even as she fired her gun on repeat.

The first bullet missed by a margin, but it was an afterthought as her second shot struck true.

McCann expected to find a bloody drilled hole into the horse's right shoulder blade. She'd also expected more of the diabolic neighing.

Instead, the horse's flaming eyes doused and its crimson stained teeth, fresh with Amsler's own meat, flushed clean. Golden skin vanished into a bubbling gorge. The horse turned into a geyser, spraying into an eruption of liquid, much of the spatter rejoining the loch.

McCann remained frozen; her gun was pointed toward nothing now. She popped off another round anyway, because she needed to.

"My God, Amsler," she wisped, finally lowering her piece and trying not to look at Amsler's mashed head.

McCann couldn't *not* look, though, and the sight of his extricated remains sent her stomach into a broil. She hurriedly sheathed her Smith & Wesson before hurling all over the ground.

***

The medics came to bag up Amsler's body along with the same Forensics team who'd been here only two days ago. District 7 Precinct Commander Shanice Baruti had left her family dinner to preside over the scene. The victim this time being one of her own.

The surviving partner tremored, even with a wool blanket thrown around her. Forensics made an off-color joke about having pulled the prior crime scene barricade tape too soon as they passed by McCann. Not one for gallows humor in a profession where it separated the hard from the soft, she tossed her right middle finger to their backs.

"Losing a partner's never easy, McCann," Commander Baruti told the detective with folded arms across her chest. "Amsler was good at his job. Damn good. This is a tremendous loss and I'm as broken up about it as you are, but what you're saying about his—passing in the field—I don't need say the claim of a horse creature was ludicrous enough coming from Hannah Baxter. From a 14-year veteran investigator, it's—"

"It's goddamned true," McCann hissed at her superior. "I'm not asking you to believe me any more than we did Hannah at first. I was here when it happened, though, ma'am."

"With *no other witnesses,* McCann," Baruti fired back sourly. "I don't need to tell you this doesn't look good. For now, you'll need to turn in your badge and firearm. I have no choice but to place you on suspension until further notice. Debriefing first thing tomorrow. I wish I could believe your fantastical excuse. I really do, but *seriously?*"

McCann let her commander have the point, knowing her future had been brutally altered. McCann would likely be let go of the force.

Worse, she could be charged with Amsler's death. She could be put away in Sheppard Pratt, judged mentally incompetent. She'd never be able to face Amsler's widow, Rina, again, despite their long friendship and despite none of this being McCann's fault.

Tuning out the chatter around her, McCann wiped away a fresh set of tears from each eye.

Her vision cleared, McCann could see what nobody else did, since they were all occupied trying to make sense of the unexplainable. The fantastical, as Baruti had correctly called it.

On the watery horizon, where the plane was slashed by the shards of sunlight dashing it, a manifestation arose. Settling atop the water, for a moment.

Even this far away, and with the fleeting impediment of the two paramedics removing a heavy black pouch containing her partner, McCann saw a horse shape turn its watery head in her direction before galloping at hyper speed across the watery plane, fizzling into a phantastic mist nobody but her saw.

Come back again, you're next, she heard a voice, death itself, taunt her as a warning.

Run

Baltimore County Forensics Evidence Item # 11

Analyzed and authenticated by: R. Morton, 9/27/2025 11:28 AM

Author(s) Kathryn (Katie) Carlisle

Last Saved by Carlisle, Kathryn

Revision Number13

Version Number

Program Name Microsoft Office Word

Company

Manager

Content Created 8/30/2025 7:54 AM

Date Last Saved 9/21/2025 10:09 AM

Last Printed

Total Editing Time 38:22:00

Running Journal – Katie Carlisle

August 30th

Distance run: 1:02 miles
Time Completed Per RunFit App: 12:37
Location: Neighborhood, Arnold Street

I don't know what I'm thinking trying to run, much less keep a journal about it. Holding myself accountable, since that's the popular thing people say when they want to meet an insurmountable goal.

Like losing 40 pounds.

This whole thing already feels futile, day one. I'm short of breath, my ribs hurt, and I nearly vomited once I stopped at a mile. The bile tasted like chicken cheesesteak, onions, peppers and hots. What I had Grub Hub deliver from Nat's Pizza last night after signing off from work. If Armageddon has an actual taste, I think a regurgitated sub with the works is it.

My knees popped a bunch of times after the cool down. As I expect it will happen in thirty years before I turn sixty. They popped again up the steps to my apartment. How does one so young as me get so decrepit?

A single lousy mile, wow, and I'm already thinking about chocolate chip pancakes and that syrup and cracked pepper coated bacon they have at First Watch. Million Dollar Bacon, it's called. I want some right now. God, I'm pathetic.

Dr. Buckner said my cholesterol is way high for a woman of 28 years and my height, which is 5' 2". He pulled no punches telling me I was overweight. Hell, my mirror told me that long before him. I'm thinking of switching plans with a better deductible next open enrollment. I should get a nicer doctor, female, one with more bedside manner, a slamming figure and someone who calls shade on those stupid medical shows that just never go away. Dr. Buckner's always bragging about his golf game to his receptionist every time I'm there, but his poochy stomach says he consumes a lion's share of red meat and beer in his own right. Hypocrite.

Yeah, screw Dr. Buckner, but he does have a point. My ass is as wide as a snowman and my thighs jiggle when I'm naked to the point I'm glad I'm not dating anyone right now. I wouldn't want to fuck me, either.

Oh well, day one, in the books. I got the run in with the temperature outside being 83, which made me sweaty enough. It's supposed to leap all the way to 96 later today, sheesh. August is over, already, come on.

I'll be a good girl and have a banana and scale back the sugar in my coffee to one spoonful instead of three. It's a start.

September 1ˢᵗ

Distance run: 1:34 miles
Time Completed Per RunFit App: 15:22
Location: Neighborhood, Arnold Street

I went a little further today, but *my time,* ouch. A one-year-old starting to get its balance can lap me at this point.

My legs were burned long before bed last night. No pain, no gain, my gimpy dad, a Gen X'er still stuck on *The A-Team* and Eighties pop has said enough times to make me believe he's fooling no one.

I hobbled my way down the steps this morning out of the apartment. The guy in Unit 103 gave me a compliment for my new running endeavor. I haven't gotten his name in the year I've lived here, but he's a nice guy I see in passing at the mailbox or in the court while taking out the trash. Black guy, easy on the eyes, kinda sexy with those dreads and his scruffy chin wag. He smells like weed most of the time, but he's in shape. He looks cut from what I can tell. Solid biceps pouring out of his usual Bob Marley, Black Uhuru or Peter Tosh t-shirts. He walks like a bulldog and the view from behind shows off a rigid butt I wouldn't mind having a private look at behind closed doors.

Back to me, as far as I'm concerned, two days doing this, I'm shitting the bed at running. Someone my age should move like a gazelle. Getting out of shape, working from home, eating like a fiend binging Netflix and Max every night? Yeah, I did this to myself. I own it.

I did watch a fitness trainer on YouTube before opening this log. Blonde, a power lifter who must've bench pressed her tits away, but she has the calves and glutes of a goddess. I forget her name, but she said we should all space out our runs, not do them every day.

Works for me.

September 3rd

Distance run: 1:86 miles
Time Completed Per RunFit App: 19:41
Location: Neighborhood, Arnold Street

The day off did me good, apparently. Nearly two miles!
Not too awful a time, either.
I'm not as sore as I was yesterday, that's a plus.
My ass is still a horror show, but you know what? It's only my third run and having cut out a lot of carbs and sugars and throwing more

kale in my salads, I've already dropped three pounds! I only need to
lose 37 more to reach my target weight.

Katie, you got this, bitch.

September 5th

Distance run: 2:68 miles
Time Completed Per RunFit App: 27:54
Location: Reynolds Park, north of Hunt Valley

I'm confessing to having a cheat day yesterday. A dozen honey
bourbon wings, two pints of Hazy Daze IPA and a brownie ala mode
for dessert. I cut out breakfast, though, and I had a big bowl full of
mandarin oranges only for lunch. The total calorie crunch I calculated
was 1600. Four hundred below the daily recommended for women,
per Dr. Buckner. It's still a win as far as I'm concerned.

I decided to change things up and drove out to Reynolds Park for
today's run. A bunch of laps around the community pond. I think
the paved walkway comes out to three quarters of a mile.

Not sure if the change of location or rest day between events was
the reason, but I killed it! Nearly three miles and only my fourth run,
I didn't expect such great results. My feet didn't hurt for once, and I
could feel myself picking up speed.

I do have to make note of this strange old coot who was fishing
in the pond. It's not fall quite yet, but he was wearing a heavy red
and black checked flannel shirt. Lumberjack couture. In 85-degree
weather! The guy had the baggiest jeans I've seen on anyone, and I
assume he's missing a belt or close to anorexia, since he kept pulling on
his britches. Britches, who says that anymore, other than my parents?
Geez, Katie, download the AARP app already!

Anyway, said old coot kept watching me as I passed by on each lap. Never waving, just sending me this doofy smile I suppose many elderly people show to fake over when their brain cogs start coming loose. Freaking weirdo.

I passed Rastaman from 103 again. He had a joint lodged in his mouth and he was carrying a fistful of grocery bags in each hand. Jesus, his forearms! He gave me a quick jerk of his head and his eyebrows went nearly up to his forehead, like he was happy to see me.

Thinking about him in bed between my legs no doubt gave me an extra spark today.

Jesus, Katie, shut up already, before this turns into amateur porn instead of a fitness log.

September 6th

Distance run: 3:22 miles
Time Completed Per RunFit App: 31:17
Location: Reynolds Park, north of Hunt Valley

Hot damn, it's Labor Day and look at me go! A 5K!
Two days in a row of distance gains and geez, *that time!* How ya like me *now,* YouTube Artemis?
I'm already feeling more like a million bucks instead of Million Dollar Bacon, even if I came home reeking and it took extra effort to get my gooey leggings off. It was already 79 degrees when I got out this morning. Fall's just around the corner, what I call my thrive season. If I'm running this good now, I can't wait to see myself in October!

Not much else to say, other than I saw that old goat at the park again. He was wearing the same clothes as yesterday and fishing out sunnies from the pond. It seemed he was getting one every time I passed by.

The freakazoid turned to me each lap and wiggled the fish, still on the hook at me. As if they aren't struggling enough on their own to get free. What a cruel bastard, even if he lets his catches go.

The guy looks like one of those bearded and busted cowboys from those archaic black and white westerns Dad loves much. Even from my higher ground on the blacktop path, I can tell the looney old fart is missing several teeth.

Eww to all of that.

September 7th

Distance run: 3:44 miles
Time Completed Per RunFit App: 34:02
Location: Reynolds Park, north of Hunt Valley

Well, only a little gain in distance today and my time isn't what I'd hoped for. The temperature's breaking, though. It was a much cooler 68 this morning. I feel I've hit my stride now where I'm hardly laboring to breathe and I'm not wheezing through my cooldown.

I dropped two more pounds, yay! Working from home's a blessing, but it's also made me horrendously fat, so now it's time to take my excesses and turn them into successes. Damn, that was corny.

Mom and Dad came over last night and brought a lasagna to die for. However, this new fitness campaign had me skimping my portion from all that ricotta, mozzarella and ground sausage. Mom's always been the best cook, and she's used to my eating heavily. I could see the disappointment on her face I'd only taken half of my usual portion of her lasagna. When I explained the reason, she looked less put-out, and then both of my parents congratulated me.

It didn't stop them from leaving the lasagna leftovers with me, though, dammit.

We're talking half a tray left. I can't eat all of that!

Maybe I'll bite the bullet and try to break the ice with Rastaman. Maybe see if he'd like to share the lasagna with me. I wonder if he likes IPAs.

For that matter, I've never tried weed before. I wonder what it's like to be high.

Only downer of the day, that nasty buzzard was there at the pond again, turning around to look at me every time I ran by him. Every. Single. Time. Worse, he pivoted all the way as I passed, switching his pole from hand-to-hand to watch me go. I checked over my shoulders twice to see he'd changed position to keep his focus on me.

No catches for him today, other than his many looks at my bubble butt.

I'm gonna find a new place to run. That guy's a full-on perv if I ever saw one.

September 9th

Distance run: 2:07 miles
Time Completed Per RunFit App: 22:19
Location: Oregon Ridge Trails, outside of Hunt Valley

New location, the beautiful hiking trails at Oregon Ridge.

While the views are spectacular and the cool, fragrant woods really agree with me, the inclines were fucking brutal, and I had to pause my running app numerous times to catch my breath. I felt like the amateur I am.

Here I thought I was getting somewhere!

My scale says I dropped two more pounds, even after eating half of the half tray of Mom's lasagna for lunch and dinner yesterday. Probably shouldn't have had an IPA with such carb-heavy food each time, but to hell with it; the scale tells me I'm doing great and I'm now 33 pounds from reaching my goal, woot!

I haven't seen Rastaman lately and I don't have the guts to knock on his door.

Guess I'm gonna end up finishing this lasagna by myself.

September 10th

Distance run: 5:19 miles
Time Completed Per RunFit App: 54:46
Location: Neighborhood, Arnold Street and Payson Boulevard

Holy shitballs, can you believe my distance and time, even without a rest day?

It's starting to feel like fall and the kids have been back in school this week, which, you know, better them than me, since high school was *so* a decade ago!

I'm excited that I'm doing my entry today before my shower instead of after. I smell like I tumbled around a horse pasture for nearly an hour instead of running, but whatever. Besides, I need to sign in to work *now* so they see I'm there "working," since my killer run today's put me way behind my usual schedule.

Five miles! Despite that trail run yesterday jacking my pulse into overload. Even with the constant stop and go at the intersections that affected my time (not too much, though) today, I'm so damn happy!

Five miles!

September 11th

Distance run:3.38 miles
Time Completed Per RunFit App: 37:26
Location: Oregon Ridge Trails, outside of Hunt Valley

Third day of running in a row, pushing my luck again at Oregon Ridge. The results were not as spectacular as my flat road five miler yesterday, but there's a huge difference between flat terrain and rugged uphill and windy everything. I stayed on a combo of blue and red trails this time, though I heard a few hikers talking about a pretty section of the trail system with a long stream. It's on the yellow trail, I think. Another time.

It's Sunday and the scale's been my friend, telling me I've lost—drumroll—four more pounds!

How is this possible so fast?

The trails were heavily loaded with people, but most were friendly and accommodating to give me passage. I felt special, in a way, since a lot of them smiled as I passed and two ladies shouted, "Get it, girl!" at me.

I may be losing it, though, since I *think* I saw that disgusting old degenerate from Reynolds Park.

I was coming down a slope on the red trail when I came across a man with his head down. Gravity was pulling me along and I was running so fast. I could be wrong, but I'd swear I saw the same red and black checkered flannel shirt! I think I saw him tugging on his pants, as before, like they were about to drop to his ankles right there in the open air.

The guy I saw today was mumbling to himself. If it was English, it was the worst attempt at it I ever heard. It was more like **REDACTED** but that wasn't what alarmed me.

He lifted his head just enough that I could see a mostly toothless man with a scraggly beard and his indecipherable gibberish turned into one of those hideous cackles you'd see from The Joker in one of those silly Batman movies.

When I slowed down long enough to turn my head without worry of slamming into a tree, the man was gone! I stopped altogether and felt my heart racing worse than my first run. He *couldn't* have gone up the slope and out of sight that fast!

I'm about to lose my mind.

It being Sunday and feeling totally snaked right now, I'm having more than a couple IPAs the rest of the day.

Get your shit together, already, Katie.

September 13th

Distance run: 5:36 miles
Time Completed Per RunFit App: 54:46
Location: Neighborhood, Arnold Street and Payson Boulevard

Street running suits me better than trails, it seems. I go longer. I go faster. I'm a porky little badass. My glutes feel tighter now instead of two large, shimmying dabs of Jello. My hamstrings are also tight and I'm having trouble stretching. More like *concentrating* on stretching. Oh well.

I got out earlier than usual today and having skipped on Monday, I felt rested. *Fired up.* The results showed.

I even ran into Rastaman, and I got his name, finally. Erik.

That's about all I got, since Erik was on his way out, but it feels trivial instead of a victory.

In fact, the elation of my whole run's kiboshed.

You know why?

I saw *him.*

I know it was the guy this time, since he was carrying his fishing pole and a plastic tackle box, swinging it like a pendulum by the handle.

The same red and black lumberjack shirt. Same baggy pants I could see him hoisting at the hip even with his fishing gear in hand.

It was at mile three, almost exactly, after I'd turned onto Payson Boulevard.

What the hell was he doing there? Reynolds Park is another three miles from Payson. Does the guy live somewhere in the vicinity, and he walks back and forth all that way?

Shit, as I think about it, Oregon Ridge is another three or four after that, right? Yeah, I just Google mapped it.

You'd think the guy would have a car to get out to Oregon Ridge, at least.

All I can say is he didn't look my way this time, but I'm all but certain he knew I was there.

Other bummer, I gained a pound back. Shit.

September 15th

Distance run: 4:22 miles

Time Completed Per RunFit App: 44:22

Location: Neighborhood, Arnold Street and Payson Boulevard

That's a weird set of numbers for you, looking at them right now. My distance time, a near-perfect replication of numeral sequence.

I'm getting upset now, to the point I can't do this running route anymore.

Hell, not even around Hunt Valley.

I'm thinking of calling the police at this point.

Yeah, like anyone's ever going to read this dumb journal aside from me, but hell, if it's ever needed as evidence or something, let the record show, by my own eyes, that damn geezer was out there *again* today on Payson. Same soggy logger wardrobe which he constantly hitches up. Carrying the same tackle gear. Is he homeless or something?

Once I spotted him, I nearly shrieked and I know it's ridiculous, but there's something wrong with this guy, I'm telling you! Seriously *wrong!*

Especially when he also stopped across the street, placed his tackle box down with such care you'd think he was carrying a mini nuke in there, and then he pointed at me. I could see his mouth open, fully blackened from the distance between us. I didn't hear anything, but I knew for sure he was laughing at me.

Like he'd done at Oregon Ridge, because it was him, I know it was!

I turned off my running app at that point and bolted back for the apartment. The only saving grace being my legs are hard and strong now. I never looked back.

Sidebar, Erik has a girlfriend. Of course he does. As I got back, I saw them both getting out of his car, her hand patting that super fine ass of his. Tall, ebony, thin, tits bigger than mine even at my fullest weight. Looking at me as if she could sense my momentary jealousy. So that's confirmed; Erik's no chubby chaser and white chicks aren't his thing.

To hell with all that noise, I'm *fucking scared.*

September 19th

Distance run:2:26 miles

Time Completed Per RunFit App: 24:57

Location: Terrapin State Park, Stevensville, MD

What the hell was I thinking?

I laid off running for a few days. Gained a couple of pounds back. Fuck it.

I'm having trouble focusing on the numbers and spreadsheets for work. Data analytics for a brokerage firm are as monotonous as documentaries on the goddamn Yucatan. I've been answering business calls on my cell phone in a crabby tone I know would get me written up if I was in a traditional office environment.

I called out today because I wanted to run, but not around here. Christ, I've been chased out of my own town in the quest to get fit.

I picked a park over the Bay Bridge at the beginning of Maryland's eastern shore. An hour ten to get there with a few road jams.

Terrapin Park borders the Chesapeake Bay. It's largely flat with wooded patches here and there, but mostly it has a set of wide-open trails threading through marshlands and open pastures. You can drop off the paths and catch some tasty beachside views of the Bay.

For a while, I'd gotten what I wanted from this trip. A level plane for running, a warm if not overly hot sunbeam in my face, a faint waft of saltwater. My lungs thanked me before the rest of my body. For a moment, it felt like a needed heal.

Having taken a few days off from running out of fear of finding that old man again, I was a little sluggish at first, but I got my rhythm quickly enough. I took comfort there were other runners there, even a few other porkers like me. We all waved to each other in transit, regardless of size or shape, like we were part of a secret club.

It was the nicest time I've had in a while.

I feel cheated for having driven so far just to take a damn run, but more importantly, I'm *terrified*.

Because? You guessed it.

He was there.

I don't need to describe him. You know what I'm going to say. It was all the same outfit and the same tackle. With all the people milling around the park and at the edge of the water, he'd somehow managed to find me when nobody else was around.

I saw he had something dangling from his line.

Not a fish, though initially I thought it could've been an eel.

It was the patters of blood dripping into the dusty path we were on letting me know this was no eel.

It was an intestine!

I swear to God it was an intestine!

He said something to me I couldn't make out. Like Oregon Ridge, it sounded like he'd **REDACTED** but I couldn't decipher it.

He laughed that hideous giggle at me, and I sprinted away, knowing he wouldn't be there when I flash-checked him.

What the absolute fuck is this, and why me?!?

September 21st

Distance run:0 miles

Time Completed Per RunFit App: 00:00

Location:

This is mostly likely my final entry because he's found me.

I'm looking at him right now through the curtains, standing on Arnold Street staring in the direction of my apartment, like he knows which one is mine. He's acting like Michael Myers stalking Laurie Strode outside her high school classroom in *Halloween.*

Exactly like that. Statuesque. Doing nothing but staring in my direction.

I heard his laughter last night when I tried to go to sleep to no avail. It was muffled, like he was outside my front door. I knew it was him.

Why I've been targeted, I'll never know. To my knowledge, I've never done anything to offend crazy old guy fishermen, but after I saw him at Terrapin Park, after all the alien-like gibberish coming out of his mouth sounding like **REDACTED** , I wish I owned a gun.

I didn't call the cops last night, but I just did moments ago. The male dispatcher sounded robotic, like he didn't believe me. He was going through the monotone motions of logging my call and allegedly an officer's on his way. No first responder, though, I already know it. I called more than 20 minutes ago. If I die because nobody took me seriously, I hope they trace my call to that smug prick transmitter.

Christ, the old man's making his move, crossing the street, heading in my direction!

Same tackle box, same fishing pole. Nothing's on his line currently, but I have a horrid picture of him gutting me, pulling my intestines out and hooking them as a trophy catch.

Please, please, please, go away, you fucking monster! Whatever you are, I know you're not human under that mooshy log splitter attire.

I'm hitting save on this document right now and if I die, I pray someone will find this. I just know you're going to **REDACTED**

END OF TRANSCRIPT

FINAL ANALYSIS: ENCRYPTED
PASSWORD REQUIRED

Chickeerun

1957.

A rock 'n roll pneumonia was being stirred up in Elmhurst by Chuck Berry from the rolled windows of Paul Hartwell's 1956 Ford Fairlane. Berry's guitar was an echoing maelstrom all around the timbered corridor leading to McDermott's Quarry. Downright satanic to the older generation, who couldn't get their ears, much less their minds around male musicians of color triggering their white offspring into a veritable insurrection.

Berry, along with Little Richard and Larry Williams ushering sparks of a discomfiting, Post World War II mutiny against traditionalist darlings Perry Como, Vic Damone, Frank Sinatra and the corny stylings of Charles Wenninger and Tommy Dorsey. Ironic, then, Elvis Aaron Presley, a white Southern boy with enough upfront manners to lead a Charm School class for men, was targeted by fundamentalist America as Public Enemy number one.

The murder of Emmett Till by the Klan in Mississippi still fresh in people's minds two years later, Berry's bop beat was not merely infectious; it was a whumping tone of aggression in disguise of blues-bombed pop inciting white suburban teens into an impromptu sock hop in the woods.

Late August at McDermott Quarry, which car jockeys and hog riders had been testing their mettle in the grand expanse preceding the reservoir for nearly seven years. Often to settle a score, sometimes with "pinks" on the line, as in vehicle ownership registrations, or dibs to a girl. Always with someone's honor at stake. The game, Chickeerun. Two opposing vehicles coming at one another head-on, daring the other to pull away first. The loser, hence, being a chicken.

Thus far, Elmhurst's seven years of Chickeerun had produced little more than dinged and scraped tail fins, driver side paint trades and busted side mirrors. Steve Conway being the unluckiest competitor who walked away with only a broken wrist and a score of bruises after jackknifing his 1950 Pontiac Chieftain. A mean feat considering how bulky the sucker was.

The only death to be told from McDermott Quarry's gladiator games of steel and horsepower, unconfirmed other than the telltale burned grass, was a young female motorcyclist from three towns over in Buckley, Francine Haney. Rumor had it in 1954, Haney had a grudge to settle with a male biker passing through with his riding gang. Nobody knew what the real beef was. All of it was speculation. Speculation that a group of riders naming their pack The Old '48s on a northbound ride ended up in a verbal scrum with Francine who all but sucked their exhaust pipes to ride with them.

If you believed the story, The Old '48s kicked Francine to the curb for being a chick. Francine took exception and called one of their gang members a chicken, challenging him here at McDermott Quarry. Nobody had seen Francine since. Nor had local police, keeping a purposeful blind eye to the Chickeerun events, been able to generate evidence of anything, other than a large patch of scorched turf long grown over. The Old '48s themselves disappeared, likely changing their gang moniker to cover up whatever had happened in '54.

The damnedest thing, which kids still talked and laughed about three years later. Did Francine Haney die that night, or had she simply vanished somewhere to anonymity like The Old '48s?

Guys and girls were joined at the hands (only two of the eleven teens being actual couples) and going to town in the grass and the dirt, cha-chaing and jitterbugging, the girls spinning into the folds of their male partners before being twisted back in release. When loosened of one another, some random kickups, scissor twists, paddle slides and hip-crashing Hallelujahs ensued like a televised swing show had dropped into the woods to film them. Headlights from side-by-side cars shined upon their earthen dance floor. Kids turning Seniors carried Berry's beat of rebellion in a final salvaging of their freedom.

Suzi Abbott and Eddie Feight, having been together all through high school, were raising dirt and hell at their busy feet, clomping and stomping in a brisk rendition of The Dog. The chain slinging from Eddie's belt loop and latching into the wallet inside his pocket swung and sang its own music against his black tweed pant trousers. His coal-colored patent leather loafers which he religiously kept shined, carried an easy inch of dust upon them.

No slow dragging to be found. WNJP was hot tonight and playing solid cookers. None of the love stuff.

Deejay, Stan "The Man" Mensah, a favorite with the local teen set, kept the airborne party rolling with his inimitable drawl, a mash of bumpkin and Bohemian banter setting off the rockabilly swing of Wanda Jackson's "I Gotta Know."

A rumble (an engine in this case, not a gang fight) of 80 horsepower sounding like a snarling wildebeest stopped the festivities in its boogie woogie tracks. A blue poly hardtop 1955 Chevy Bel Air. Its handler gave the car a hard wildebeest rev as an exclamation point to his entrance. The party was *really* about to start.

The dancing gave way to whoops and cheers as kids scattered to fetch cans of Schlitz and Hamms beer from their cars. A ricochet of popped and spritzed tops went down the line before many (the guys, especially) guzzled instead of sipping to relieve their raw throats.

The music gave pause for Stan "The Man" to drop a sweltering forecast nobody paid attention to. The heat was here long before the new arrival to their gathering. Sweat stains were found all over blouses and button-downs, most evident upon Eddie Feight's plain white short-sleeved undershirt. The few girls who'd worn silk scarves had long ditched them. Nearly all of them smartly wore thigh-hugging shorts or calf-stopping Capris.

"Pete's finally here!" Sally Ketner chirped. Sally being the only one in sight wearing a fluffy sky-blue skirt. Her dance partner, Bill Reinheimer, had daringly lifted her into the air earlier, giving all the hound dog guys a treated flash of her ruffled sky-blue panties.

"Fashionably late as always," Sally's former boyfriend of a mere month, Richie Acevedo added, sending a loud tremor of laughter even the sharpest ears in the Elmhurst town limits might detect. Richie had been dancing with Peggy Green all night but staring lovesick at his old flame more than Peggy.

"As late as that Francine Haney girl," Peggy nyukked. "She's *real* gone!"

"Bad taste, girl," Sally needled Peggy.

Their tradeoff drifted to the wind, since the celebrity of the hour had made his grand entrance and there was no room for gossip of potentially deceased cycle girls.

The driver in question, Pete Spears (a name he wore like a badass) let his 350 V8 4 speed engine idle as he ran a comb over his freshly gelled wave, parting the back of his brown neck length strands into two separating pitches overtop the collar of his black and white pattered bowling shirt. The shirt being left unbuttoned down to his plain white tee covered navel. Pete's Vitalis-held duck's ass do was as notable around Elmhurst as his custom '55 Chevy.

Leaning against his Fairlane, reedy arms folded across a solid black button-down short sleeve, Paul Hartwell hollered "Fifteen minutes, to be exact, Spears! I was beginning to think you were gonna punk out!"

"My ass, Hartwell!" Pete shouted back with a hoisted middle finger meant to be playful instead of malicious. The two had been friends since fourth grade elementary. Before tonight, the worst they'd done together was set off a string of firecrackers beneath the hairy butt of a scrawny Schnauzer as ancient as its owner, Lawrence Jenkins. The mustachioed mutt aged 12 and stupidly named Clyde never saw his thirteenth year. The prank had gone south as Clyde inexplicably caught fire from behind and had the equivalent of a canine heart attack. Both Pete and Paul's parents ended up paying out restitution to old man Jenkins. The entire episode was an infamous Elmhurst scandal.

"No, you can sit on *mine,* dickhead!" Paul dished with a dirty salute of his own, as if there'd been no such thing as a dead Schnauzer to hang between their consciences.

It was Paul's car carrying the tunes, and this time, Buddy Holly with his backing band, The Crickets, strummed the plucky intro to the balmy "That'll Be the Day."

No one picked back up in dance mode, but Cookie Webster had the quote of the hour by saying, loud enough to be heard overtop the grumbling Bel Air, "Buddy Holly and this music will live forever."

"Rave on," said the thick hipped Harriet Cotterman, who bumped the nonexistent hip of her twig of a date, Ted Sizemore.

Ted nodded in agreement with everyone else as Pete finished the last few passes on each side of his greaser spread. Paul Hartwell detached from his regatta blue over snowshoe white top Fairlane with his half-finished Hamms, gliding into a knee-bent strut some people thought was cool, others totally square. Either-or, it was the apparent signal for everyone to flock to the side of the Bel Air.

"You wanna call stakes on this?" Paul asked, gently pushing past the crowd so he could reach his uplifted palm into the Bel Air.

Sliding his downturned palm along Paul's in a gesture of camaraderie, Pete said, "You could get me one of those brews if you're any kind of man."

Paul grinned and pointed at Cookie Webster, snapping his fingers like an order instead of making a polite verbal request for her to jet back to his Fairlane and fetch another Hamms.

"You might want to do something about that nervous twitch, Pauly," Cookie snarked at him.

"Women," Paul uttered sarcastically, keeping his face turned to Pete. "You'd think they'll want the vote sometime. In all seriousness, though, you want to drop a friendly wager on this?"

Following a snicker-snort at Paul's initial jab, Pete said, "Nah, man. Just bragging rights. I'm undefeated and after tonight, I'm gonna stay that way."

"As *you* said, Spears, my ass."

"We'll see, Hartwell."

"You're going down this time, like that Francine Haney chick, whatever ended up being her fate. She lost, I'm sure."

"Oh, please, not even the big, bad myth of Francine Haney intimidates me. Especially some dame. Not on her best day, no fucking way. Besides, she rode a hog. You think she'd be able to stand up to *this?* Pfffft."

After all the sizzle over the radio, things finally settled into a romantic coggle with Sonny James waddling a serenade to adolescents more interested in a car duel than hearing about their young and muddled first love with pretentious airs of true devotion and deep emotion.

"I brought two, Pauly," Cookie Webster chimed, sounding more like a brag. "I figure you might want another one for yourself to get your balls up."

"Thanks," Paul sneered, grabbing both unopened cans of Hamms and passing one to Pete, whose sudden gunning of his engine served as his lip-silent expression of gratitude.

Together, old buddies opened fresh beers and bumped them together in a toast. Froth spilled out of each can onto their respective man's fist.

"We really gonna do this, man?" Pete asked, slurping on his knuckles, then the Hamms, taking down nearly half of it in two huge gulps. He belched afterwards like it was part of his charm. "You still have time to back out of this, Pauly."

"You're the one who called me a chicken. We're doing this."

"I was only fucking around. I mean, look—"

"We're doing this," Paul repeated, tilting his head back and pounding his beer to the raising of a "Chug! Chug! Chug!" chant from the others. Except for Cookie, who was glancing over at Pete while shaking her head in disbelief at Paul, who added, "Don't screw me over, Spears."

Pete repeated Cookie's head shaking gesture. "Alright, man. It's your funeral."

"See ya later, alligator," Paul taunted back with a dry smirk intended to hide his sudden nervousness. There was no hiding, however, the sudden flush on his cheeks in contrast to his blanched skin which had showed a rowdy suntan moments ago. He spiked his emptied beer can to the ground with an artificial bravado.

"After a while, crocodile," Cookie finished the exchange before Pete could.

"Let's get it on!" trumpeted the dateless Frank Mullen, who bolted into the scene, whipping a weathered, floppy Red Sox ballcap off his head. A hat Frank had worn to such excess the red "R" logo on the cap had become frayed. This being a rarity for him to be seen anywhere in Elmhurst without his Sox hat on, Mullen was already showing a way-too-young sign of a receding hairline.

"You look like you're getting a hard-on from this, Mullen," Paul scoffed with a lurch in his voice, the first true sign of his fearing what was coming.

"I'd like to ride with you, Pete," Cookie said, pushing Frank out of the way and leaning deep into the Chevy, enough for Pete to catch the iris, jasmine, rose bergamot and patchouli blend of her heavily doused Jacques Guerlain's Shalimar. Cookie's mousy brown bouffant hadn't been fazed by the dancing earlier. It was locked even firmer than Pete's duck's ass. Her blazing red lips bespoke of sin Pete immediately hoped to capitalize on.

With nothing more than a backwards jerk of his neck by way of invitation, Cookie toodled around the Chevy and let herself into the passenger side, slamming the door from exuberance.

"You sure you wanna do this," Pete said to her instead of asked. He was scoping the slopes of her heaving breasts he knew were authentic, not the augmentation of those stupid missile tit bras American women were so fond of these days.

"If it's okay with you."

"You may want to belt up, then. I can't promise what's gonna happen and I sure don't want your death on my conscience."

"Meh," Cookie dismissed him with a nonchalant wave. "Seatbelts are for my folks whenever we go anywhere in that dreadful Edsel of theirs."

"Hey, how old are you, anyway?" Pete quipped, feeling a slight numbing of his stirring loins with sudden panic. "I know I dropped out two years ago, but I can't say I remember what grade you were in then."

"Be cool, Pete," Cookie returned. "I turned 18 two months after graduation. I have a job in a typing pool, 25 hours a week, at Sun American Life Insurance. I'm still shacking with my parents until I save enough money to get out on my own."

"Where would you even go?"

"Burbank, California. Done deal in my mind, baby. Come with me, if you like. The racing's hot out there, I hear."

"I don't race," Pete said flatly, "and California's for surfing. I could've palled around with Jimmy Dean, I reckon."

"If he'd lived," Cookie added. "Total tragedy, that guy."

"Right. I have to ask you, though. Is Cookie your real name?"

"Anna Mae, but I despise the hick sound of it. My family's originally from Detroit, so the country girl thing doesn't fly with me, you know? I eat a lot of Spritz and Crispos around the house, so my mama planted the 'Cookie' tag on me. Better than Anna Mae any day."

Frank Mullen interjected by waggling his Red Sox cap for attention as Paul Hartwell's Fairlane pulled up behind him.

"Alright guys, you know the rules," Frank squealed, so into the moment he looked like he'd gone back in time to the final threshold of his waning childhood when *Captain Midnight* first aired on television.

"Yeah, yeah, yeah," Pete cut him off.

"On my go, you both head in your opposite directions, then come at each other. First guy to veer off is a chicken. I love this stuff!"

"Try *doing* it once, punk!" Paul yelled from his car.

Pete laughed at that, stamping on his gas pedal while keeping the Chevy in park.

Paul returned the gesture, not quite as loud as Pete's car, but with longer decline from the rev.

"Ready, boys?" Frank asked, crouching into a full squat.

"Oh, for Christ's sake, Mullen," Pete groaned. "You'd think this was a drag race."

"Idiot," Cookie added with a limber nod Pete found sexy. He was already long past this moment, one that could cost his, Pete's and Cookie's lives. He was already calculating the quickest way into Cookie's lime green Capris.

Frank propelled himself into the air with his Sox cap raised overhead, but neither guy started off until Frank brought the cap all the way down to his waist like a starter flag.

Both cars initially ground into the grass from the sudden acceleration, each struggling for traction. Paul sent Pete his coolest, most confident glance. However, as his Fairlane fishtailed a moment, Paul suddenly looked like he was considering staying straight and bolting out of the quarry altogether.

As Pete drove what he estimated to be a couple of hundred feet away, navigating a spread of trees marking a perimeter around the scene of engagement, he turned the Chevy around and paused to make sure Paul had done the same thing the further down.

"Last chance to bail," Pete told Cookie, not looking at her, but ahead, wondering for a second if this was what knights felt like jousting. Crammed with adrenaline, heartbeat pounding like a Buddy Rich snare roll, the beginnings of an erection puffing inside his pants.

"Go ahead, baby," Cookie whispered, apparently sensing what going on with him downstairs. She slid her left palm onto his thigh and cupped his package through his denim. Her sudden rubbing was enough to send Pete's penis into a full scream. He kept pressure on the brake, tapping the accelerator a few times, then flicking his headlights twice to signal Paul it was time to come at each other. Paul sent back a deuce of flickers of his own.

"I had a total crush on you before you quit high school, Peter Spears."

"Not now!" Pete exclaimed. "This shit's life or death! I need to concentrate!"

"Whatever you say," Cookie said in a sour tone Pete could've cared less about. The moment she let go of him, he stamped on the gas and rocketed the Chevy forward.

Paul was already on his way. A quick glance at the line of beaming headlights to the side showed all the onlookers clapping and cheering. Frank Mullen looked like he'd ball Pete faster than Cookie would if he'd let him.

Pete felt his chest flood as much as his manhood and for a second, he couldn't breathe. It was the same thing every time he'd played Chickeerun, except for having company in his flirtations with suicide. This challenge against a longtime friend being his sixth duel. Assuming they survived, Pete was quietly thrilled to know his victory lap was a locked-in sinking of the pink.

That was the thing, though.

They needed to survive.

"Come on, man!" Pete growled as the cars bore down upon one another, headlights penetrating each other's windshields. In a crazy hurry, it was difficult to see his opponent. "Turn away! Turn away!"

"Yeah, Pauly, don't do something stupid!" Cookie added, grabbing for the dashboard.

Neither of them had been paying attention, but Don and Phil Everly were lamenting the end of romance over the AM radio in perfect synchronized harmony. Bye, bye to love, hello to loneliness. The Everlys shared an ironic, bittersweet sentiment of wanting to die.

For a moment, it looked like Paul was about to hold the line as his headlights drew closer, closer, frighteningly closer. The grille of the Fairlane looked like iron teeth eager to chomp instead of being caved in. That's what Pete focused on to get his sense of bearing where Paul was. So far, Paul was anything but a chicken.

"Pauly, pull away, damn you!" Pete screeched. For the first time feeling he would finally lose in this reckless game of death

Yet it was Paul who faltered, swinging hard out of the way with the barest time to avoid a collision. Pete's Bel Air narrowly missed clipping the rear of the Ford club coupe as he roared past without incident.

Paul's hasty turn sent him into a wild ninety-degree spin, his spinning whitewall tires trying to grab and slow him down without rolling the car altogether. The Fairlane bobbled backwards after the grassy skid until Paul got it to a full stop.

"Whooooo!" Cookie squealed. "What a rush! I can't believe we nearly died!"

Braking the Chevy without planting full-force, Pete was about to join in her celebration until he saw something just ahead, feet away.

What in God's name?

It was a girl.

Nobody Pete knew. Nobody Cookie and his younger friends likely knew either.

She wasn't dressed in your typical feminine gear. No skirts, slacks or blouses. She had on a black leather jacket and hip-hugging pleated jeans overtop thick-shanked motorcycle boots. Her auburn hair was pulled into a ponytail beneath what looked like a beige Bronson motorcycle cap. She was a female Brando circa *The Wild One*.

"Holy fucking shit!" Pete hollered.

Now he stomped on the brake as the girl came closer into view. Cookie fell forward against the dashboard. She'd barely had enough presence of mind to thrust both hands out to shield herself from a face plant into the windshield.

"My God, Pete, what are you doing?!?" Cookie shrieked, pushing back into her seat.

Outside of the Bel Air, there was a snarl to the newcomer girl's face as she put out a hand covered inside a black leather glove. Just as Cookie had done to save herself. In this case, the unknown girl's hand raising motion was intended to make Pete stop as the Chevy came directly at her. The tires were failing to grab into the loosening earth beneath them.

The closer he got to the girl, the more Pete could spot burn marks scoring her right cheek, down to the neckline. Her jerked back ponytail was streaked with black on the same side of her burned face. Whoever she was, apparently a biker chick, she'd been given a vicious lick from a fire kiss.

What she was doing out here on their turf was secondary to the fact she was in the way and refusing to move.

"Get outta the way, you crazy broad!" Pete screamed, wincing as he bore down on her. Squeezing his eyes tight as the Bel Air ground into a long, dirty skid to halt, he failed to see the girl gnashing her bloodstained teeth at him.

Expecting a thump against the car and nothing coming from it, the car finally stopped. The smell of hot burning tire rubber fooled Pete for a moment into thinking he'd hit the girl.

But she was nowhere to be found.

Hurriedly shifting the car into park and sweating down his chest, Pete whirled in his seat to face Cookie.

"What the hell happened just now?" she blared, swatting his shoulder. "I could've fucking died from *that* after barely dodging a crash!"

Pete was more shaken than angry at Cookie's strike, and his voice, once full of bluster, proved it. "Tell me you saw her!"

"Saw who? Pete, what's wrong with you?"

Shifting his stare into the rearview mirror, there was nothing to be found other than the other kids running into the field, some heading in Paul's direction. The others galloping towards him. The surrounding woods captured their euphoria and sent it back in an encompassing echo. Like they'd been frolicking high in the trees instead of ground level.

"Jesus Christ! You didn't see that girl just now?" Pete bellowed, feeling his spine drenched. His eyes were watering like he was about to cry. He wouldn't do that, however, especially not in front of a girl. "Biker chick, part of her face all burnt! Don't even tell me you didn't see her! Don't you dare!"

Cookie cringed at his exclamations as the car rocked and the sound of metallic slapping along the roof, trunk and the hood with cheers of encomia barged through Pete's still rolled-down window.

Frank Mullen, of course, was the most emphatic. "Still undefeated!" he roared, like the win was as much his as Pete's.

Neither he nor Cookie paid attention to the raucous hoopla. Both of their eyes were filled with fear for different reasons.

"Who do you *think* it was, that Francine Haney person? Oh, come on, Pete! Have you gone insane?"

***

Every American town had a Makeout Point and Elmhurst's was a set of bluffs off Bakerfield Road. It was spotted half a mile from the Nickerson farm, taken over by the senior high school set. There was a passed-along agreement shared between the local teens, town fuzz and the surprisingly tolerant Nickersons themselves. The latter two would look away from any shenanigans in the way of drinking, toking and screwing, so long as the whole debouched bonanza was over with by 11:00 p.m. Come what may for any transgressions beyond said hour. The only time the town police had to arrest anyone at Makeout Point that wasn't related to ordinance, underage drinking or illegal possession was to bust up a switchblade rumble involving two gangs from the nearby borough of Steinway. If you want to call the three-man Aces squad versus the four-man Raptors crew actual gangs.

Right now, there were five cars at Makeout Point, a silver and black two-toned '54 Buick Century, a 1951 Oldsmobile Super 88, another '56 Ford Fairlane (red and white paint scheme this time), a '56 Ford Sunliner convertible with its tarp roof raised up and, of course, Pete's Bel Air.

Everyone was lined up with a single file but spaced apart to accommodate privacy amongst themselves. The unspoken but well-known law of dibs was first show got you center spot, hence easiest backout for departure.

Another unspoken rule at Makeout Point was you kept car-to-car socializing at a minimum. The name of the spot said it all. Nobody was out of bounds for stepping out of their cars to view the night sky, getting some air or taking a whiz in the open field. Sharing beers, bumming smokes, quick catchups amongst friends who knew to keep a low voice, also fair game. Otherwise, shaddup and keep your sex howls in check. Simple courtesy.

Anyone coming to Makeout Point had one music style in mind and Dean Martin was not on the menu. Thus, the collective wisp of WNJP floated through each car (three of them already wobbling on their axles) and encircled the entire gathering. Already out for around five years, Paul and Paula's "Hey, Paula" was still a station mainstay and swooning over the action right now.

"You sure you've come down from whatever you were on, earlier?" Cookie questioned Pete from her side in the backseat, already unfastening her bra beneath her blouse. "I don't judge if you do hard stuff. It would explain that crazy flipping out earlier."

"I don't do that shit!" Pete sneered, blowing a secondhand Marlboro puff towards the front of his car. The nicotine cloud took a wild swing to the left and out of the front driver's side window.

"Cool your jets, space cadet!" Cookie shot back at him. "No need to get testy. I'm making sure you're alright. You didn't say one word until we got here."

"I know what I saw."

"Then let me be a distraction," she said, slipping her blouse over her head to reveal a bounty of breasts, the nipples already hard.

"Damn," Pete said in awe of her, shucking his bowling shirt, then pulling the collar of his white undershirt out and up to avoid being singed by his cigarette, finishing the entire removal with the smoldering stick still in his mouth. He tossed the shirt to the floor and sent a cloud of smoke with a creak of his lips to the side.

"Will you finish that damn thing so you can kiss me? For crying out loud, why do guys think it's sexy to smoke and fuck at the same time?"

Pete snorted in laughter, the first time he'd relaxed since the Chickeerun, since the biker girl showed up.

Was it even a biker girl? A real, human biker girl? Francine Haney was never confirmed to be alive or dead. If it was Francine, then—

Cookie was already out of her Capris and bottoms and tugging on Pete's fly.

"You don't waste time, do you, lunatic?" he chirped, finally distracted from thoughts of burned cycle girls, real or not.

"Foreplay's a waste of time."

Pete sucked the remainder of his Marlboro and in the process of arching and twisting to flick the lingering butt out the car window, he clumsily bumped his crotch against Cookie's face.

"Alright, alright, spaz!" she jeered, tugging his jeans down to his knees.

"Sorry," Pete returned with a coarse giggle still clogged by his smoke.

Cookie was doing a contortion act of her own, throwing herself halfway into the front of the Bel Air, her bare creamy buttocks rippling back at Pete, "Yeah, yeah, enjoy the view."

"What're you even doing?" Pete asked her, sending his remaining clothes to the car floor.

"Looking for this," she responded, spilling back into the rear of the car, then smiling wickedly as she looked down at Pete's revealed boner. "Wow, someone's happy to see me."

She wiggled a single wrapped Co-Ed condom before tackling Pete.

They slurped each other more than kissed. They grabbed one another like the Commies had given fifteen-minute advance warning of an imminent nuclear shower across the United States. Hard, ham-fisted, all but desperate to cum.

"Here," Cookie told him, grinding her hips with nothing between her as she ripped open the condom package using her teeth. She pulled the gooey latex ring out and passed it over to Pete.

Whether it was overeagerness or a defect in the product, Pete had the rubber on for three unfurls before the elastic tore down the left side of his member.

"You gotta be fucking kidding me," Pete wheezed, more in shock than anger.

"Ohhhhh, nooooo," Cookie moaned, slapping Pete's outer left thigh.

"It wasn't my fault! Where'd you even get this, out of one of those coinboxes in the guy's room?"

"I pinched it from my brother Steve. He hasn't been lucky these days, so, you know. I doubt he'll ever catch on since he has an entire stack, the poor schmuck. Oh, Jesus help me for what I'm thinking."

"What?" Pete quipped nervously, eyeing his extension then Cookie, who was already lying back against the seat and opening her legs.

"Take me raw," she told him with a blend of anxiety and lust. "But you need to pull out when you're ready, Peter, or I'll kill you. I'm not on the pill."

All Pete heard was "Take me raw," as he was inside of her and deep so quickly, she squealed and winced at the same time.

Stan "The Man" Mensah might've been an eye in the sky that second since he was ushering Elvis back to the airwaves with Presley's poke along cover of the old standard ballad, "Blue Moon."

"Hey, take it easy, King Kong!" Cookie protested, even if it was minor sentiment between her moans of ecstasy. Her right breast flopped back and forth against her cheek. Pete clawed her left one as he pounded his groin into hers, fast, hard. Straight lined and on the edge, just as he drove in a Chickeerun.

Pete's rushed strokes went against him, however, and he couldn't control himself. His guttural, prolonged grunt was no doubt heard amongst the other cars.

"Oh, my God, you bastard," Cookie whispered in shock. "You *bastard,* I told you to pull out!"

"I—I—" Pete panted, still inside of her, still shuddering.

She managed to hoist her right foot backwards beneath Pete's chest and with force matching a blow from any guy Pete had taken (better than, honestly), she kicked him off her.

"YOU BASTARD!" she shrieked, enveloping herself with her head down so she could muffle some of her crying.

It didn't work as they both heard "You two alright down there?" from one of the other cars. A female laced with a cutesy Brenda Lee swill.

"Yeah, thanks!" Pete shouted back, looking down his raging dick, then at Cookie, whose ribcage heaved in and out from her sobs. "Look, Cookie, I didn't think—"

"No, you didn't!" she fired at him through her soaked, spit slung lips. She raised herself to her knees and launched her palm against Pete's face. "If I get pregnant because of your dumb ass—"

She didn't get to finish the thought as Pete returned her a smack, backhanded, double the force.

"Don't you ever fucking hit me, bitch!" he roared, getting up in her face. "You hear me? Ever! Get the hell out of my car!"

He was already pulling his underwear and jeans back on, a shaking, primeval animal in doing so.

Cookie, naked and stunned, blood trickling out the left corner of her mouth was so stymied by Pete's actions she could only squeeze out, "What?"

"YO!!!" a burly male voice, deeper than a teenager should have, roared one car over. "You're wrecking the mood, ya apes!"

"Shut up, already, all yas!" came further down the row.

"You need help down there?" chimed the only compassionate voice. Brenda Lee's shadow.

Pete was dressed in everything but his shoes and those he left on the rear floor as he dove for the front, snatching Cookie's clothes faster than she could process what had just happened. She was too hurt, too confused, too betrayed to stop him.

Adding her purse on the passenger front seat, Pete tossed the entire bundle out of the driver's side window.

"You can walk the fuck home," he derided her with a frigid tone matching Reverend Rinaldi's denunciation and burning of comic books in Corpus Christie, 1948.

"No, you can't do this," Cookie blubbered back at him, splaying her hands in desperation. Her nudity had been beautiful upon revelation, centerfold worthy. Now, her slumped shoulders sent her breasts into a flaccid, defeated slouch. Even with scant lighting inside the car, her makeup had turned into disastrous clown streaks. She would only titillate sado freaks in such a state.

"I mean it. Get out. Don't make me pull you by the hair."

"Pete, you're not this evil, come on." So abrupt had Cookie's fury wilted into despair.

"Get out."

Trembling like the car had dropped thirty degrees inside, Cookie clambered into the front seat. Her thighs shook worse than her bottom, her breasts compressed, released in a less than erotic jiggle, than smashed against the vinyl and cloth upholstery of the passenger seat. She had her hand upon the silver window roller to steady herself as she pulled her knees over the seating backrests.

She took one final look at Pete, the same Pete who'd been several different Petes this evening. Right now, the flare in his pupils and the callous twist of his wrist to start the ignition showed Cookie a Pete she wished she'd never jumped into his Bel Air with. Cruel, immoral. Not a mere cad, but a villain.

Acceptance of her fate restored Cookie's defiance even as she opened the passenger to let herself out, naked as a jaybird.

"I'll get you for this, Peter Spears."

He said nothing. He just waited for the door to shut before he angrily shifted the car into reverse, the rear tires digging into the dirt, then outright screeching like the announcement of a criminal's getaway as he slammed the gearshift into forward and roared off.

"I'LL GET YOU FOR THIS!!!" he heard in his wake. The Cadillacs were in apparent cahoots with him as they doo-wopped their way through the rapid-fire "Speedo" over the radio.

Pete roared down Bakerfield Road with their whumping rhythm lofting inside the Bel Air. He gritted his teeth and pursed his lips, wondering if he'd gone too far just now, not knowing the time but figuring it was long past ten. If anything, it was getting close to 11:00. Which meant Sheriff Drayton would be making his nightly sojourn over to Makeout Point soon.

He eased the accelerator for that very reason.

Also, to reconsider turning back for Cookie. Yeah, he'd fucked up while they were getting it on. The last thing he wanted in his life right now was a goddamn kid, especially as a 50-hour a week mechanic at Mickey's Garage back in town, renting out the spare room in the back at $35.00 a month.

"Shit! he hissed, smacking the steering wheel. The Cadillacs were done with him. Sam Cooke took their place, crooning, lovestruck like, to all of Elmhurst about his current flame who just sent him. Honestly, she did.

Pete let the car go even slower, down to the country backroad posted speed limit of 40 miles an hour.

He was thunderstruck with indecision, feeling guilt for the first time tonight and he gave voice to it, uttering, "I'm a goddamn jerk."

Bakerfield Road had been empty all this time, another four miles from the Elmhurst town limits from here. Thus, Pete hadn't the faintest clue, even lingering right next to him, he had company.

"Oh, my fucking God!" Pete shrieked when he finally detected the whitish blue haze surrounding someone on a motorcycle.

The Bronson cap had been replaced by a riding helmet, the visor covering the rider's eyes. The burn marks down the slender jawline and the waggling remnants of a lady's ponytail were a dead giveaway.

It was *her!* The female rider from McDermott's Bluffs!

Francine Haney.

"It's really you, isn't it?" Pete wisped, stomping down on the accelerator and gripping the steering wheel with both fists as he felt a slight wobble towards the right in the alignment.

She was still showing in his side mirror, still in the opposite lane. Intermittent white dividing marks whisked behind him on repeat as he climbed in velocity to 55 then 60.

A flash check into the rearview showed Pete the same scene, only the girl ghost was catching up on her phantasmic motorcycle.

"Fuck me," he tremored, suddenly knowing the panic Cookie did moments ago when he'd ditched her.

65. 70.

And there was the cycle ghost, back alongside him. Her ponytail flapped even harder as she matched his speed. How could a ghost mimic reality like that? She *was* a ghost, right? She had to be dead, given her burn marks and that garish glow around her. The ultimate loser in her own game of Chickeerun in '54, now a goddamn ghost.

As if to think ghosts were real, *come on!*

"Francine?!?" Pete shouted out the window, looking at her, then forward, then back again. They had the road all to themselves. His stomach began to hurt nearly as much as his sticky balls. "Francine Haney?"

He knew he'd struck gold by the hideous smile sent back to him. This close, Pete could see the dried blood and char along her teeth, making the burn marks down her face more apparent.

"The fuck do you want?!?" he caterwauled, now at 75 m.p.h. He'd be into town in no time at this speed.

Then what? He'd get to the garage and his rented room and hide? From *this?*

Francine Haney creaked an alarming undead smile from atop her menacing 1950 Triumph Thunderbird, which he recognized. The cycle could reach top speed at 100, he knew. The same as his Bel Air.

Yet somehow, something beyond the mortal world, thrust the Thunderbird faster than your typical drag launch. She was suddenly down wide open Bakerfield Road a quarter mile, just like that.

Francine kept going, gaining further distance from Pete, who had to lock his grip on the wheel so tight he thought his knuckles might burst through the skin.

"Jesus," he groaned, now faced with the decision of slowing down again or keeping up this speed. Was Francine heading into Elmhurst to lie in wait for him, whatever it was she wanted from him?

Pete didn't have to wait for an answer.

As fast as she passed him, Francine on her Thunderbird was coming back to him. On his side the road this time. She was a blue, hazy rocket streaking for him.

Her intent was to play Chickeerun.

"You can't be serious," Pete said. Those were his final words conjoined with Larry Williams' madcap screeching about a girl as skinny as macaroni. Bony Maronie was the hip chick's name.

Praying he would simply run through the ghost girl as he did at McDermott Quarry, that ended up being Pete Spears' last prayer in life.

God never got the message. Or if He did, He left his summary judgment right there on Bakerfield Road and moved on to the next petitioner.

As his Chevy lifted into the air and barrel rolled twice upon contact with the ethereal entity, Pete's car exploded in midair.

The last thing Pete saw before a vortex of fire took him gone was the mounted miniature license plate atop the Triumph's front wheel cover.

Engraved upon it was **U LOSE 57.**

Lucky Burns

Audrianna's fist hit the desk with the same venom a current day video gamer did smacking the shit out of an Xbox or PlayStation controller, stuck in a rut from a Boss level adversary, unable to move upwards to the next level. No matter how many gimme chances with endless respawning, the stakes were different, but the repeated futility made for similar explosive outbursts.

"A turndown in nine minutes?!?" she exclaimed, feeling a sharp pain jettison through her right wrist, her lead hand. One already showing the introductory signs of carpal tunnel syndrome. Those everyday aches annoyed Audrianna. So did the twisting barbs inside her knees which often woke her up at night and the constant squelching inside her guts warning at the possibility of developing irritable bowel syndrome. At age 48, she wasn't old, but Audrianna was already feeling the early going signs. Traces of gray slashed through her sloppily pinned mousy brown hair, adding years she didn't yet own. Wrinkles at the corners of both eyes were duplicated at the edges of her mouth. She never knew Grandmother Abigail, her mother's mother, but the pictures left behind by both women told of a premature aging gene it appeared would strike a third generation.

All of this with menopause heading around the bend, yay.

The sudden flash of pain in Audrianna's wrist gave her something to gnaw on, something she could relate to. "Did you even read the story, for Christ's sake? You *people* must be the same A.I. you forbid in your submission guidelines! You couldn't even be professional enough to capitalize 'Author!'"

With an unintentional fanning of the flames, Harriet Wheeler of The Sundays swooned a maudlin Nineties alternative rock rhapsody through the desk speaker connected to Audrianna's laptop, mewing with her assured finality here's where the story ends.

"Fanning the flames, heh," Audrianna joked to herself, since there was nobody around to hear her shade-calling rant, much less her private tomfoolery. Well, there was her cockapoo, Sam, who was peeking his head into her office right now, assessing the situation. If Audrianna had been looking at her cocker spaniel-poodle hybrid with his floppity black ears set to a fluffy white body, she would've seen indecision pooled across his scruffy, bandit masked face. Concern, even.

She jerked her left desk drawer so hard it made her coffee cup lilt off a cork drink holder. Amazingly it had held the line during her calamitous pounding. At least there'd only been a swig left inside the white ceramic mug initiated by the black stenciled scrawl **"PUBLISHED AUTHOR HERE."** Audrianna had bought it for herself 12 years ago as a totem celebration when her horror story, "Feeding Time" had been picked up by an upstart press, Carpathian

Massif's debut anthology, *From the Verges of Făgăraş*. She'd been paid twenty-five bucks and a contributor's copy, spending half her earnings on the mug.

The sound startled Sam, who pulled his fleecy little head back and retreated with a scamper to the studio apartment living room.

Inside the drawer was an unwrapped spare pack of Post-It Notes, a slubbed pencil in need of sharpening, a half-chewed pack of spearmint gum Audrianna hadn't touched in nearly a year. Bookmarkers and business cards from authors she'd met but never followed up with to network and a handful of thumb drives, some loaded with her stories. The others contained downloaded cell phone pictures of a former life when there was still a man who claimed to have loved her, Lane.

Set to metrics, the mini measurement of a crumbled life.

The other items in the drawer were four Bic lighters of assorted colors, powder blue, sunshiny yellow, cherry red and basswood green.

It was the latter one Audrianna snatched with the same pulsing hand. Normally she would hit the ibuprofen after such intense pain. For now, she was eating the immediate throbbing with the same delight as her nightly bowl of vanilla ice cream stacked with a chopped banana, walnuts, coconut shreds and that old-time gooey Bosco chocolate syrup she'd developed a taste for in her early twenties.

Audrianna hit the spark wheel of the Bic with a faint grin, even as her thumb sent a backwards flare through her extensor tendon into the digitorum. She grunted in reaction, wishing the emailed rejection of her latest story, a horror yarn titled "Convalescence" set inside a haunted hospice center, was a hard copy print letter.

She could set fire to it right now, in the bathtub where she could douse it and promptly wash away the remains. A proper healing process for a writer having chased her passion for nearly three decades with bragging rights to only a handful of accepted short stories in magazines, websites and anthologies. Plus, a print-on-demand collection of her terror tales only 23 traceable people bought titled *Lucky Burns.* More than half of those came from her distant relatives. None of whom gave her feedback.

Burn, baby, burn, just as she'd done for years with every single canned rejection letter snail mailed to her. Sure, some writers held onto their elimination-styled correspondence as motivational pieces, things to look back upon and scoff at once they'd finally made it. Not Audrianna.

There were times she looked forward to the rejection notices, even when they came months after her submissions. Setting them ablaze wasn't just therapeutic, it was her royal fuck-you to editors who'd never see the intended gesture anyway. Torch and flush, move on. Try again.

This time, however. This was a new precedent. A fuck you in the face of the artist right at the gate. No laminate, no passage. VIP only.

Nine minutes. Nine *stinking* minutes after she'd hit send on her submission to *Dancing Macabre,* she got her so-called evaluation and swift dismissal. This wasn't just frustrating, it was insulting. Like telling millennials their smart phones are more organized than their actual lives. Instant trigger.

"I followed your guidelines," Audrianna hissed, letting the flame douse for a second before reigniting it. The flare from the linden tinted Bic shared the wealth with her thumb. Accordingly, Audrianna's agitation rose. By now, a seasoned response sequence. "I was thirteen hundred words below the five thousand cap! I tightened the story on purpose with that specific count in mind! I edited it three times! The one-inch margins are correct, it's all in Times New Roman! Jesus fucking Christ, I followed the William Shunn format to the tee! Nothing that should've given me an automatic dump! I'd have more respect for you worms if you'd given me the California no instead!"

Audrianna released her hold on the butane button, then stroked it right back on again. She could hear the faint hiss-whoosh even over Jane's Addiction's "Summertime Rolls," which had ousted Harriet Wheeler's doldrums in favor of their trundling lust for life.

Audrianna turned away from her laptop screen, which currently showed the completed manuscript of "Convalescence," and stared at the wriggling flame.

The esoteric community would call it scrying, but Audrianna had no interest in finding spiritual divinity and magickal enlightenment within the flame. Fire was sacred to her, yes, but it was for purging and purification purposes, not spotting combustible salamanders and fire deities. That stuff was more for Salem and the Dark Fantasy crowd.

"You suck," Audrianna jeered herself, extinguishing the lighter again. Her thumb gave thanks for the reprieve by easing its pounding to the usual dull twinge she lived with every day.

The lighter was hot, and she sat it down on her desk. She hadn't noticed Robert Smith of The Cure caterwauling his way into her eardrums through his snarky tirade against the pretentious farts of the world, "Why Can't I Be You?"

"You suck!" Audrianna shouted this time, glad for the soundproofing of her two-bedroom studio. Gladder for the framed picture she seized her gaze upon, like a security measure. A picture of herself with her favorite horror author, Nancy Collins, she'd had taken at Terror Jam VIII four years ago. Nancy had been everything Audrianna had hoped for in meeting her. Patient through Audrianna's rapid, nervous spooling over her project ideas and request for suggestions on how to get more publications. Advice had been given along with an autographing of Audrianna's copy of Collins' 1996 Sonja Blue novel, *A Dozen Black Roses*. It was a glorious day.

That was then and four years later, Audrianna had only nabbed two publication offers, a web journal that didn't pay and an anthology which later wheeled the story back to her after their crowdfunding efforts failed.

Everything else, rejection.

Rejection.

REJECTION!!!

The assuaging Nancy Collins photo could only delay the inevitable.

Without hesitation, with full intention, Audrianna slapped herself.

Left hand, left cheek. Audrianna knew the moves of this ugly solo tango. They were instinctual at this point.

Then to the right, she slapped that side. Even distribution, when it came to serving herself pain. The prolific if tormented Robert Smith could have done the same to himself somewhere in a venerated career of gloom worship. Possibly during the recording of *Pornography*, considered by many to be the most dampening album of any genre. "You've *always* sucked!"

She'd already deleted the rejection email from *Dancing Macabre*. Nowhere near as satisfying as burning, though. Click and disappear, big whoop. It took longer to wipe herself clean in the bathroom.

Audrianna couldn't set her laptop on fire. Wouldn't. That would be utterly insane, but she wanted to just the same, like all the words it had taken in transcription from her hungry, impulsive fingers was to blame for her endless misfortune. There was no other scapegoat, manifest or immaterial.

She'd set lots of things on fire in her years. As a teenager, it had been harmless stuff, dead autumn leaves, castaway burger wrappers in gutters, fliers she ripped down from telephone poles. Just because. Audrianna had taken to the crueler invective of incinerating ants and spiders, thinking nothing of their throes of insectoid agony other than wondering if they actually screamed.

Later in life, Audrianna took her lighter to paper towels and the coinbox tampons in the ladies' room during her lunch breaks when she'd worked as a post compliance associate for Fairview Federal Savings and Loan. It was more satiating than eating. The burning helped her focus in a highly tedious and eye-dulling job filled with proofing for document conformity, number accuracy and compliant signatures accompanied by proper notarizing. She took her lunch later than the rest of her team, volunteering to take the latest shift so she could eat for show, then do her burning business in the rest room sink. Once Audrianna had finally been caught by department manager Shiela Orr, she was fired. Apparently, the bank had been biding its time for the right excuse to let Audrianna go, since she'd been given a letter of termination on her way out the door. She'd burned it, of course.

It was burning low score school assignments when Audrianna began to correlate fire with eradicating her ongoing shroud of inferiority. Which she still wore today as readily as her cuddle dud violet fleece bottoms and Vampirella t-shirt. Printed comic art across the black tee featuring the iconic, amatory Nosferatu vixen from outer space courtesy of Patrick Berkenkotter, who'd illustrated Nancy Collins' run on the series.

Maybe it was because of Audrianna's cigarette smoking father's love of snapping the lid to his sterling silver Zippo lighter, for no reason at all, other than it calmed him down when he was in a crappy mood. And as a single dad to her for nine years before he'd forced her to move out, he'd been in a constantly crappy mood. Also, maybe because of the time the miserable bastard had crushed her entire world telling her she was wasting her time trying to be a writer. Rubbing salt in the wound by calling her a homely plain Jane who'd have to work extra hard to land a guy and make it in this world.

"You fucking hack!" Audrianna raged further, slapping herself again on the left side. Then the right. Then back and forth, each crack crying of the despondency and failure she felt.

The real crying followed, and she blubbered through her anguish, grateful Lane wasn't around to see this. He'd already seen enough to break up with her. Bad enough the burning incidents spanned unpaid bills and parking fines to an eviction notice Lane had to bail her out of.

The final straw for Lane came from Audrianna's reaction after his telling her, as people in their forties, she needed to get a better grasp of her finances. She supplemented herself with menial, barely making it work cleaning homes and small offices, plus walking dogs while spending most of her free time writing in a fruitless pursuit of glory. Lane also said she needed psychiatric help, and he would help figure out a way to pay for treatment since Audrianna carried no health insurance. In a fury that scared even her, Audrianna told him to piss off with a virulent growl through her teeth before taking a lighter to her forearm. Her screeching had jolted him. Her masochistic laughter thereafter pushed him gone forever.

Audrianna muted her cued classic alternative rock playlist on Spotify with a click of her wireless mouse, cutting off The Mission's "Beyond the Pale." It would be the last song she'd hear. Ever.

"I hate you, Dad, but you had a point!" she lamented with a self-loathing whimper she hated herself even more for. As if a woman hitting a critical milestone 50th birthday should be acting like a spoiled child. "I've pissed away so much of my life chasing down a dream!

I've wanted this since I was a teenager! I didn't expect success then, but for fuck's sake! Writers half my age and double my talent are getting noticed, getting out there, getting published! I'm a goddamn pretender! I can see it now! I've skated by, I've needed help at times, and I had Lane then, but of course, I screwed *that* up like everything else in my wasted life!"

Audrianna snatched the Bic again, already cooled, and set it alive.

She didn't hesitate.

Kids always loved to play that silly game of Can You Take It? holding their hands overtop lighter flames, bragging rights coming with the one who could get closest to the biting flame without pulling away.

Stupid shit with forgettable incentives.

This was for real.

"AAAAYYYYYYYIIIIEEEEEE!!!!" Audrianna bellowed after palming straight onto the lighter's minute conflagration. She could hear the sizzle of her skin and knew by experience how quickly the skin was splitting, singing, reddening and ultimately blistering.

Sam galloped into her office, his toenails scratching along the wood finish of the hallway. It was amusing on other days. Nothing funny between them this time, and Sam sent his human a combined woof and whine of concern.

"Mommy's alright," Audrianna said to the petite dog in a voice as shaky as her scorched, clawed hand. "I'm alright. I'm better than alright, because now I know the truth and what I must do. Where I must go. Wanna come with, baby boy?"

Audrianna held the stirrup of Sam's leash inside her right hand, gauzed and still tremoring. She'd used no healing ointments nor taken any other precautions. The wrap was simply to have enough grip on the leash.

Inside her left hand, Audrianna clutched a yellow 24-ounce bottle of Ronson lighter fluid like it was the second most important thing in her life behind Sam.

Which used to be writing.

Audrianna had parked in the furthest reach of an abandoned parking lot nobody else was around to challenge her for.

There was a hefty breeze in the September air, the kind hinting of a harsh winter. Strong, but not so blowy you didn't want to be outside in it. Not yet. With a hoodie or a jacket, it was comfortable. The kind of breeze that could be the best friend of football quarterbacks and place kickers for at least two quarters of a game. A possible added adversary for the other two.

It was a breeze which suited Audrianna's purposes. A breeze which seemed to understand her, like lighters always had.

She'd driven out to a left-for-dead strip mall, Blueberry Bluffs, every single unit emptied, a slate film cast upon many of the windows. Some oddly had help wanted and for lease signs left taped to the glass doors. She hadn't come here often during its heyday, but Audrianna could remember chain shops like Nautica, Banana Republic, Chanel and on the less bougie end, JoAnn Fabrics and Payless Shoes. A local Ohio pizzeria bearing the grandstanding name, New York's Finest Slice and a banging barbecue joint called Chubb-a-Dubb's used to be here. The expected dash 'n grab familiars like Starbucks, Chipotle and Subway also once holed up here. Audrianna was all but sure there'd been a karate dojo she couldn't remember the name of. Only that it had reminded her of the goofy chop sockey soap opera, *Kobra Kai,* which she'd been addicted to for five seasons but wouldn't be around to see its sixth and final.

All of it, gone. Relocated, some outright folded.

Audrianna had seen many deserted commerce centers like Blueberry Bluffs profiled by internet bloggers taking pictures of vacant strip centers and what people called "ghost malls." Shelled, scabrous, dismantled, forlorn shades of their one-time commercial splendor.

Another victim of the advocacy of online shopping, the emptied shell of Blueberry Bluffs was an L shaped, decayed string of cleared out brick-and-mortar stores. A gaping cavity upon the world left to rot without the dignity of refilling. Instead, forsaken and left to Mother Nature, already showing signs of her reclamation, judging by the sprouts of crabgrass Audrianna could detect along the storefront sidewalks where people had traipsed as their daily-do only a few years ago.

The entire scene of disregard, an expression of how Audrianna felt. Rejected.

This was fitting.

The omnipresent cracks in the blacktop of the Blueberry Bluffs parking lot looked like garish tarmacadam veins and that was from her ground level view. Tendrils of green were already peeking through here, too. Audrianna took a moment to wonder what view the birds had.

"Sam, my man," Audrianna said with a sigh, her eyes filling up once again as she unhooked him from his leash.

A low peal from the dog told her he was confused as much by her letting him loose as he was what the heck they were doing in a horrible, festering place like this.

"I've done right by you, best I can, even if I didn't get your shots done regularly. You can do better than me, though. I'll always love you. Thank you for being the only living thing who didn't think I was utter shit."

Audrianna uncapped the Ronson container, which she'd ordered through Amazon a year ago. For the silver Zippo lighter inside her pocket. The only memento of her father she'd kept after his death by COPD nearly a decade ago.

The tears came again, and Sam took a cautious step in her direction, putting out a paw and poking it at her twice, his canine way of asking what the living fuck she was doing.

Audrianna tilted the lighter fluid and squeezed, pooling her shoes, then up and down each leg. She got to her abdomen, then her breasts, homely things that they were, she scoffed at her long-gone father.

She got both arms covered as the Ronson bottle drew close to empty.

Quickly hoisting the bottle over her head, Audrianna soaked her scalp before it made a squibbed squeal through the salve before sending out air. Funny how it sounded like "RON-SON!" Audrianna squeezed the bottle again twice and got empty huffs before chucking it onto the pavement.

"Dear Editor," she said, no longer looking at Sam, who pushed his paw at her repeatedly, spiking his whines to outright barking. If she wasn't resolved to her course, Audrianna might've heard the anxiety in his voice, like he was saying in dog-speak, "No, you anthropoid fool! Don't do it!"

She smelled of butane and the oily substance had already soaked through to her skin. Audrianna hoped by calculating her dousing, this would be over quickly. She was counting on it. After all, fire had been her friend for a very long time. One of the very few of Audrianna's self-flogged life which wouldn't make it to a fifth decade.

"Note my capitalization of 'Editor.' Meant by way of respect, which you seem to have little of. So very few of you do. I have read your robotic rejection and regretfully, due to the volume of similar ones I amassed in a dead-end career, yours became the breaking point. Too many of us want the same thing. We can't all be Stephen King. We can't all be Anne Rice. I tried my best. I got to meet Nancy Collins, so I'm content. I even got my copy of Paul Tremblay's *The Cabin at the End of the World* signed, one of two days in recent memory I felt like I had genuine hope. Nice guy. He gave me more appraisal in the quick minute I chatted him up about my work in a large line of other wannabes. He'd never remember me, though, no more than you will, Editor. The problem is me. I've always known it; thus, I'll take the blame for my own nothingness. Carry on smartly, *Dancing Macabre,* you automaton bastards."

Sam barked for all his tiny worth before howling a heartbreaking goodbye and sprinting towards his uncertain future.

His shadow was lit by a nightmarish orange hue illuminating Blueberry Bluffs Shopping Center like Hell itself.

***

A year later, a story hit on the breakout Discovery Channel show, *Ironic, Isn't It?* hosted by Ryan Gosling.

It was only a quick two-minute segment which spotlighted a long aspiring 48-year-old author from Amherst, Ohio, Audrianna Newburg, who'd set herself on fire inside an abandoned shopping center in the nearby municipality of Oberlin. Audrianna Newburg was profiled as a never-made-it writer who'd set herself ablaze after the release of her POD collection of horror shorts titled *Lucky Burns* had tanked.

The segment painted Audrianna as a perpetual loner with no known friends, her aunts, uncles and cousins spread all along the west coast, and only one serious love interest in her life. *Ironic, Isn't It?* solicited a testimonial from Lane Viscuso, Audrianna's boyfriend of less than two years. Viscuso illustrated a picture of a conflicted woman desperate to be loved, having had no children, nobody she hung out with, no quickly accessible family and only a few short-term sexual partners well before him.

She was as passionate a lover as she was a writer, Viscuso said. He also described her as "ambitious to a fault and irresponsible when it came to her finances and holding down a steady income." As related to her gruesome suicide by fire, Viscuso nodded grimly and swatted away a tear on-camera while conveying stories of her arbitrary self-abuse. Incidents of slapping herself, hammering her fists into her stomach and ramming her head against her desk or refrigerator were frequent, always when she felt criticized or unworthy. Especially when she got rejection notices to her writing, and there'd been many of those.

Audrianna's obsession with fire was what concerned Viscuso the most. "She'd flick those damn lighters on and off all the time, sometimes in bed," he said. "That's some scary stuff to wake up to in the middle of the night. I cared for Audrianna greatly. I loved her, enough to offer to put her on my health insurance plan so she could get the help she obviously needed. You can imagine how that proposal went. She'd told me I was no better than her dad and she forced me to watch her burn her forearm. I'm still not over the whole thing, almost three years later."

Audrianna, having lost her mother to cancer when she was nine, was raised by an obtuse, subjective and downright mean father, Viscuso recounted. "Her dad screwed her up for life, there's no getting around it."

What would have made Gosling's narrative even juicier was the immediate spike of orders for *Lucky Burns* after the episode first aired. A recent sales count reported by the over-the-moon print-on-demand publisher, Phright Phactory, showed 27,198 hard copy units sold. A runaway best-seller by their small press standards.

Widow

She wore the road like a third skin, that being behind her tattoos, of course. Normally I preferred my women with silky, virgin skin and brunette instead of a dirty blonde, ink-slung showcase, but I was hardly turned off in this case. Her world-traveled fatigue was a second thought compared to a luscious smile that could've seduced Beelzebub himself. Even Satan could never have fathomed someone hotter than his fieriest wet dream like Alexsandra Mundy.

When I first got started as a rock journalist, I never saw a day like this coming, one where a famous (famous as far as the underground leagues went, anyway) female metal singer would break the ice with me a week before a scheduled interview session, then show me her full warmth prior to answering a single question.

I've interviewed more than three hundred musicians over the course of a decade in the life with maybe ten percent of my guests being female. The ratio is better than it used to be in metal music. Alexsandra Mundy was the exception to the rule about never mixing business and pleasure between musicians and the press. Most cases, artists strive to shield their private lives from journalists, whether those entail debauchery or monotony. Generally speaking, no musician today, metal leagues or other, wants to be branded a crasher and burner in the public eye. Don't be fooled by anything I say next if you're aspiring to write about music; this does *not* happen as a rule of thumb.

Because I'd been in the music business a while and had paid my dues through the work-for-free rags and online hubs, I became, in due time, a paid professional writer. This, on top of my full-time (and far less interesting) job as a real property clerk at the Baltimore County Recorder of Deeds, since the writing gigs were hardly enough to float on. The adage, if you're in the scene, is there's no money in music. Fact for most unless your name begins and ends with Beyoncé.

To a certain degree, rock journalism is the same life as most young bands cutting their teeth and skinning it on tour. Of course, some bands paid to play, even in these more enlightened times, since there were as many bands as there were lawyers, all scratching about for compensation and often going pro bono just to make a rep, if not a dime.

I was still single, though I'd found regular company last year in the bed of a title company recorder named Candy Cassidy before she fell for one of those pro bono lawyers I mentioned a second ago and she quickly married her way out of that racket. No advance notice on her part. She simply stopped coming by with deed and mortgage filings and she answered only one of my texts to ice our fuck buddy friendship. Too bad, since Candy's a master of verticals as she is of fireball shots at Happy Hour.

After Candy, I'd hit a protracted dry spell. I was busy slinging questions at musicians in my downtime and all but one of the women at my day job were old enough to be my mom or aunt. The exception, Kelly Jackson, was only twenty-nine and she'd already spit out a brood of three. I was amazed how trim her ass and hips had remained after knocking out a trifecta, but I'd stopped sneaking silent stares at Kelly long ago, since she adored her husband as much as her kids. The longer I go without slipping the ring on someone, the more I respect those who actually enjoy being married.

All just as well, since being a rock journalist is a lonely trade like any other form of writing. It demands freedom. To be tied down now would mean less road dogging and having maybe a quarter of the time necessary to turn in my assignments before deadline. At times, I hanker for the cuddly companionship Candy once provided me. She's into superhero flicks, which prompted the one date that didn't finalize between the sheets. It was me, Candy, and half a theater full of action junkies marveling at Captain America. Candy held my hand and sucked the popcorn butter off my fingertips, but that's as heavy as things got that night. Frankly, it was nice, and I wish things could've gone further between us, even if Candy was more into Blake Shelton than Rob Halford.

Still, there's time. I'm only in my mid-thirties, after all.

Alexsandra Mundy came to *me* with a quick hello at Facebook, of all things, considering she had a massive following with her band, Grit City Deviants. Alexsandra was maxed on Facebook friends, so we were never officially linked up online. Still, her message to me had been brief, albeit inviting:

"Looking forward to meeting you in Philly on the 5th."

Like everything else that happened afterwards, this simply did not happen as a norm. Most musicians field so much press it's amazing if they remember you down the road, much less extend such congeniality outside of the proper forum, without the leash of a publicist.

The band's press wrangler, Frannie Julius, with whom I'd enjoyed a long professional association until recent events in the shattered The

Grit City Deviants camp, set me up for an interview and show comp. Frannie said Alexsandra had requested me specifically when scanning her yet-to-be-confirmed interview schedule and she'd seen *Thunder* magazine on the itinerary.

The assignment would otherwise have gone to my New York colleague Jenny "Nuke Girl" McCann, who wasted no time razzing me as a "fart knock hack" by email after I'd landed the interview. This, of course, had nothing to do with her being a big fan of The Grit City Deviants. We're good though. I have a standing lunch date with Jenny when I go up to Manhattan next month. I'm not sure I can get into the details of my Alexsandra Mundy encounter with her, though. In fact, I know I can't, even though that'll be the first query leaping off Jenny's pierced tongue. Jenny plays for the other team, if you get me. She'd eviscerate me right there on 47th Street before the pregame Irish Curry Fries arrive at The Mean Fiddler.

I've been around the scene for years now, eight with *Thunder* magazine alone, and I've had a lot of unique interviewees in my career. Trust me when I say Alexsandra Mundy was *the* most unique guest I've ever put a recorder in front of.

She'd been traveling under the alias Tina Tottenheim, which Frannie had alerted me to in advance. The desk clerk at the Philadelphia Airport Marriott confirmed they had a Tina Tottenheim staying there after I plunked down my ID. I found out soon enough The Grit City Deviants had arrived by bus, not plane, go figure. Following a quick call upstairs to confirm my credentials, I was told "Ms. Tottenheim" was staying in Room 713.

I remember a lot of chaos going on inside the Marriott, mostly generated by a traveling team of co-ed teenaged athletes. They were doing what teenage athletes do, constituting a lot of cussing, belching and tearing down the corridors of their respective floors. You could watch their antics full hand from the open glass elevator which gave a sprawled view of the hotel's atrium and octagonal floors.

As I took my ride up, I saw one beefy jock type on the third level with a football point forward with a "go-long" indication as another one sprinted down the corridor. The ball bounced off the latter's fingertips, crashing into the rack of a young girl (possibly a cheerleader if she wasn't on a girls' volleyball team) who looked mighty pissed by the whole thing. She had excellent reflexes as she maintained possession of her interception and subsequently took a mean shot at the nuts of the errant receiver with the pointed end of the football. Alone in the elevator, I enjoyed a good rip after cringing at that dumb dude's misfortune.

The seventh floor was on the top level. Club level. Those staying there had access to the hotel's exclusive lounge, which included complimentary coffee, soda, fruit, snacks and continental breakfast. There were also more computers in the club room than on the lobby level, where the fight for user time was far more intense. I'd enjoyed such accommodation myself on quite a few assignments, the last one being in Richmond, Virginia. By rule, I carried my laptop with me on long hauls, but Philadelphia was only an hour and a half from my native Baltimore suburb of White Marsh. Thus, I was traveling light this day.

As I got off the elevator, I nodded to a balding man with a scruffy beard who was dressed in soggy Wranglers and a wrinkled black button down strained at the waist from his heaving paunch. He had on a big belt buckle with a bucking bronco branded upon a silver oval, and his belly was nudging it near horizontally. He came out of the club lounge with a pack of barbecue chips and a Diet Coke stuffed inside his chubby mitts. He looked exhausted but returned my salutation with a double-chinned nod. I guessed (correctly) he was a long-haul band bus driver. Given all the touring ensembles I've met, he wore his role like a weathered junction sign.

When I knocked on the door for 713, there was Alexsandra, looking road flogged in her baggy gray sweats and a cotton black wife beater shirt with a flaming skull and crossbones strained across her swollen bosom. In public she wore enough makeup to constitute her as a Cover Girl of the damned, but I was seeing her stripped down. Later, I'd see more. Or less, if you will. Her eyes bore puffy dark semicircles beneath the pupils and there was a trace of redness about them as well. She'd been close enough to kiss me at the door. Her breath smelled like Cool Ranch Doritos, and I instantly wanted to probe my tongue down her aftertaste.

Raining down both of her sylphlike arms and into her cleavage was green, red and yellow ink from the cavalcade of tattoos etched upon her. Part of Alexsandra Mundy's fame was her full-body artwork, which found her featured in numerous tattooing mags and websites along with metal music-themed periodicals. Zigzagging down the inner slopes of her breasts were a set of green claw marks dragging faux blood trails behind him. If she'd been balling a Martian, the kinky bleeding effect would've been sold perfectly.

"Come on in, Russ," she told me, dragging the suite door which groaned and hissed at its full strain. Pretty soon, that would be me.

I offered Alexsandra my hand for a shake, which she accepted. A nice, firm grip which commanded respect. Even with all the skin ink, I could see her biceps flexing. Some men are put off by ladies with strong handshakes. Not me. I enjoy getting on the same playing field with anyone I meet, regardless of sex.

"I appreciate your time," I told her, as I have every single guest I've interviewed in the past and still do to this day. Yeah, it's ritualistic, automated, even, but it's also professional. I believe most people today are presumptuous in many avenues of life, though I'll admit there's a slacker nuance to the lower tier music world which propagates the myth it's wholly devoid of formality.

Regardless of what happened between me and Alexsandra Mundy, I've always made it a point to maintain convention until a proper flow eases things between me and my interviewees. Since Alexsandra, convention has been more my m.o. than ever.

"No worries, guy," she told me. "I brought a few Cokes over from the club lounge. Want one? I can spice it up with some Jim Beam Devil's Cut if you like."

It wasn't the first time I'd been offered refreshments by my guests. I've probably saved a small fortune in beers from all the freebies I've been given backstage and on tour buses. A few times, I've even been offered a toke, though most musicians are as protective of their grass as their time signatures. This was a precedent, though. Nobody had offered me hard liquor, even as a mixer. If I was still green, I would've declined.

"Perfecto," I said, as Alexsandra grinned warmly, offsetting the general air of fatigue about her.

"Grab some couch, be right back."

I took a seat and opened my carry tote, which had my digital tape recorder, camera and small spiral notebook with eleven questions for Alexsandra penciled in it. I watched as she moved methodically out of the living room area of the suite and admired the gentle wiggle of her buttocks making themselves known amidst the loose cotton fabric attempting to buffer them. The waistband was draping low enough beyond her decorated hips to show no undies hugged around them, not even a thong. She was perfectly commando underneath.

Alexsandra returned with two cans of soda and a fifth of bourbon that was already half demolished. As she leaned down to hand me a Coke, for a split second, I plunged my eyes down the open cut of her sleeveless tank. However, I wanted to stay pro, which did not constitute gawking at her scrawled-over goodies. Quickly, I flashed my gaze straight into Alexsandra's eyes. She sent me a wrinkled, knowing smirk. I'd been busted.

I spritzed open my Coke and looked away from her for a moment, feeling embarrassed. I heard Alexsandra open her can and then I felt the Devil's Cut bottle nudged between the gape of my lap. Where Alexsandra had placed it, it looked like an erect glass phallus.

"How was your drive?" she asked, as I took a deep breath, suddenly aware she was toying with me. I must reiterate nothing like this has ever happened in my rock journalist life before and I doubt it ever will again. I'll make sure of it.

I won't lie; I'd fantasized about something like this hundreds of times over the years. I'd lulled around in bed many sleepless nights after a few private cocktails, slovenly daydreaming about having a backstage or rock n' roll hotel shag. That, or meeting some anonymous girl on the floor at a show (a "concert girlfriend," it was called these days) who would hunker up to me and grind my aching hard-on with her ass through our jeans while we enjoyed the show. The latter would likely never happen in my life, since more couples were attending shows together than ever and thus the concert hall has become a thinner dating pool. Besides, that sort of promiscuous behavior between strangers was more akin to raves than heavy metal gigs, at least not since Ratt and the Crue had hits on Billboard.

"I got out early," I said, trying to stay cool as I untwisted the cap from the fifth. I took a few gulps of soda virgin before gently tilting the whiskey into it. Then I offered to do the same for Alexsandra, who took me up on it. "I-95 was light for a change. It can be a real bear at the tollbooths, but I flew today. I even had time for a cheesesteak at my favorite joint on Broad Street. It's true what they say about the steaks in this town."

"Well, I'm vegan, but whatever does it for ya," she replied, taking a hit from her soda after I'd jazzed it up for her. "I know what you mean about traffic woes, though I never drive the bus, of course. I always hear Gus complain about the 'Godforsaken tolls' along the east coast. He's staying in a room on the opposite side of the floor. If anyone needs his rest, it's Gus. Can't be having any Cliff Burton repeats, you know."

"Yeah, right. Big man, heavy, horse on his belt buckle?"

"Nailed it."

"We crossed paths. He looked zonked."

"Right," Alexsandra said. "The rest of the band is in the room next door, while the crew sleeps on the bus. Of course, they're all at the venue right now, setting up the stage. We had to rent our own lighting for this show since the venue's reportedly fritzing. I need to get down there in a couple hours for sound check, but I'm all yours until then."

My entire body flooded with excitement after she'd said that, though I could never have anticipated the lengths Alexsandra would take me following such a subliminally flirtatious statement. I didn't find any overt innuendo from it, not *then*, at least. I reached for my recorder and thumbed it on. "Guess we'll get started," I said, suddenly as nervous as the time I'd bumbled my first question as a rook in front of Iron Maiden's Adrian Smith.

"It can wait," Alexsandra said, motioning for me to shut off the recorder. "Let's chill a minute first."

"Sure," I said, feeling stupid. No doubt *sounding* stupid.

"I always did like Philly. People here are deep into music, and I could get used to that on a regular basis, even though Tybee Island, Georgia is where I call home these days. As you probably know."

"A few ways east of Savannah."

"Spot-on, you know your geography like you know your tunes."

"I got drunk there once in younger times," I said, letting a guilty grin seep across my face. "Me and a couple of college buddies I haven't heard from since those wild days of shitfaced. We went to Savannah first and after baking our asses off, even with all that kudzu and hanging moss for shade, we figured the beach at Tybee would cool us off. Dumb thinking, there. That part of the Atlantic's no better than a hot tub during the summer. Smallest beach town I've ever seen outside of Dewey, Delaware."

"I'm impressed," Alexsandra told me, taking a swig from her spiked soda can. "You're not as countrified I am, but you have Tybee down reasonably accurate."

"Well, me and those same dudes only hung out on the beach for a few hours and bailed since there were nothing but families and locals who obviously didn't want hell raising college guys around. The ocean was hot enough to cover our piss, so we left our gratitude in the water and found a bar to kill the rest of the day and night in."

"Foul, but funny," Alexsandra smirked without laughing. For a moment, I thought I'd divulged too much about myself. It's bizarre to me now to think how comfy I'd become with Alexsandra in so short a time, and vice versa. I needn't have worried then, since she gently motioned for me to continue talking.

"I think we got a few miles out of town before we parked behind some abandoned gas station and slept there until we were sober enough to drive. We nearly got caught by a cop who'd been cruising by, but if he'd seen us at all, he cut us a mega break and kept rolling. Those guys and I—damn, we did some crazy stuff back then. Wish they'd kept in touch over the years."

Alexsandra nodded a couple times, surveying me with eyes that looked earnest one second, calculating another. "I've learned in life, Russ, especially being a metal singer with a small bit of prestige, most friends are *fake* friends. If those guys were your real buddies, they would've stuck by you, no matter how old y'all got."

She'd said "y'all" with every bit the "countrified" platitude she'd claimed before inquiring, "What're you, around 36, 37?""Yeah," I said, trying to be cool but knowing, a couple weeks later, I probably sounded dorky. "One of those."

"Ah," Alexsandra said in a flat tone. "That puts you one or two years ahead of me, depending on what you'll admit to. Hell, I thought *girls* were flaky about that. Age is just a number, Russ."

"Alright, sorry, make it 36 and hoping the next four years are hot rockin' before my midlife launch."

"Well, now we're getting somewhere," she said, letting her expression ease as she tilted back the soda can once more. "We've just met, but I hope after today we can be friends."

"As long as we're not fake, right?"

"Right on," Alexsandra said with a light chuckle as she reached over and patted my thigh twice before putting her soda can on the coffee table in front of us which already had an empty plastic water bottle and a half-eaten Hershey bar on it. "Come on, you *have* to the see view of the airport from back here."

I started to grab my soda and again Alexsandra stopped me.

"Leave it but bring the booze."

Again, she departed the living room, only brisker this time. The lady could cast hotter than Jimmy Houston on his birthday.

On the far end of the suite, I squinted as blaring sunlight from the bedroom splintered my eyes. Alexsandra had left the curtains opened far apart. Her bed was still made, though she'd obviously been laying down on it before I'd arrived, given the random creases atop the comforter and the stack of the pillows shoved against the headboard.

"When I was a kid," Alexsandra said, "My daddy used to take me to the airport in Atlanta just to watch the planes come in and take off. He'd always buy me a little bag of Cheetos and himself a bag of peanuts. We'd just sit there quietly, enjoying the rumbles of takeoffs and those sleek-sounding whooshes of the descents. I still love those sounds. It's controlled chaos."

"Yeah, my folks took me to Baltimore-Washington International a lot when I was five since it was cheap entertainment," I replied, feeling more at ease, though I should never have let my guard down. "Maryland homies call it BWI."

"I know," Alexsandra told me, waving me over to the window in her bedroom. "We've come through there for gigs in D.C. See, I know enough native jive to say 'D.C.' instead of Washington, D.C."

"Or worse, the District of Columbia, like an old fart politician would," I joked as my eyes adjusted to the stark sunlight.

Outside, the Philadelphia airport was about half a mile away and the tarmacs were on the opposite side of the terminal, so we didn't see any planes actually touching down on the runways, but we did see them swoop in and swoop out. The hotel was remarkably soundproofed as we commented to each other how you could barely hear the planes in action. To this day, I'm still astonished how easily we fell into sidetrack conversation. Of course, I'm now convinced it was all by design on Alexsandra's part.

"You know, another thing my daddy used to take me to a lot was bars," Alexsandra told me, resting her hip against the ledge near the window and folding her arms beneath her chest. She continued to glance outside the window as she spoke. As I said, tattooed women customarily weren't my thing, but the sun beaming across her inked skin made her fucking magnificent. It even brightened her matted dirty blonde strands to summon a glow that wasn't there in the lower-lit half of the suite.

"I'll bet you were popular amongst the barflies," I said with a chuckle.

"Hardly," she returned, shooting a quick stare at me, then back out the window. "I'm sure there were a few child molester freaks who relished the thought of plucking my seven-year-old cherry, but most of the time, I was resented."

"Was your old man aware of it?"

"Maybe, maybe not. After my mom died, he and I were inseparable. Only when I was in school, and he was at the factory working, were we *not* together. He didn't start drinking until after my mother passed, maybe six months later when I guess the reality of it hit him like a two-ton press. I would sit there quietly, nursing polish dogs and Dr. Peppers while he knocked beer bottles gone and said, 'Dead soldier, *salute*,' after each one."

"Dr. Pepper, nice," I said with sincerity. Despite having Coke that day, I'd cut soda out of my diet to help get rid of a soggy waistline which had pestered me after the Candy Cassidy affair had been terminated. Yet the thought of Dr. Pepper at its mere mention put me into a happy place I know Alexsandra picked up on. She held her hand out and wagged it in the direction of the Devil's Cut I had brought with me.

She took a long drag after I passed it over and her teeth shivered, coming within inches of clattering. Her tongue darted around her lips to swab the hot residue of the whiskey still dribbling along them. Then she handed me the fifth back, jiggled it by the neck and told me to take a hit as the remaining contents swished and gurgled as if a goldfish had gotten trapped and inebriated inside. It wasn't a stern, commanding voice she used, but one that, having already begun floating with the proverbial sheets, insinuated, *"Catch up with me, already."*

I obeyed, of course.

"The first time my old man gave me a sip of his beer at that grody watering hole in Decatur he loved more than he ever did my mother, Mack's Tavern," she went on, "the bartender, Gladys, called the owner over and we were thrown out. My dad was liquored up and he challenged the owner to fight out in the street. He got a good punch in, but that was about it. I watched my father drop to the pavement after taking a handful of shots from the owner. I'll never forget that goon screaming he wasn't about to lose his license 'over some lush who should know better than to corrupt a minor.' I've never told anyone from the press that before. Wanna know something else?"

"Of course," I said, trying to keep my voice even-kilter. Inside, I was bursting from Alexsandra's profound trust in me.

We watched the planes in silence for a few seconds, and then Alexsandra closed the already short distance between us.

"I like your writing, Russ," she said, leaning her face close to mine. Her breath was steamy and rank from the alcohol and Doritos, but my nostrils were riled up nonetheless. They demanded my pecker get with the program. "Your interviews are always interesting to read since you avoid those cookie cutter questions the amateurs ask. I get sick of *answering* them, much less reading them in other interviews. You get people to open up, and I never feel short-changed reading your work. As soon as I saw *Thunder* on our press sheet, I told Frannie she was fired if she didn't book you and only you."

"I'm flattered."

"So, anyway, when I was of legal age, I went back to that Decatur shithole, Mack's. The same lady, Gladys, was still tending bar. Kinda pathetic, you know? She looked a hundred years older than when I'd last seen her and my having grown up, out and getting a big start on my inks, she never recognized me. I ordered a Jameson shot and a longneck, Newcastle, maybe, who the hell knows. Semantics. I waited patiently for a while and remember threatening to bend the fingers backwards of this assclown who came up, put his arm around me and asked if he could have a 'close and personal' look at my tats."

Alexsandra paused there and her eyes darted back and forth within her crimson-streaked pupils, growing forceful as she drove her stare into me. I can only describe that gawp as a more frantic yet equally hypnotizing impression of James Earl Jones' Thulsa Doom. For a moment, I nearly sagged to the floor where I stood. She had me. I was transfixed by Alexsandra and recollecting it now, I'm positive she was savoring her mystique over me, judging by the brief upwards creak of the corners of her mouth. A dirty grin if there ever was one. I wonder now just how many guys she'd subdued in similar fashion over the years.

"After that creepazoid slithered away like the coward he was," Alexsandra resumed, "I asked for the owner, just to see if it was the same guy as when I was a kid. Sure enough, it was. He'd heard me asking for him and he came over to my side of the bar. I can't say time had been kind to him, either, the fat slob. Once I knew I had the right guy, I put a twenty down to cover my bill—and with a pretty generous tip, I might add—then I emptied my beer as the owner leaned forward to introduce himself. It's like he was asking for it, you know? It couldn't have been easier."

Again, Alexsandra stopped for a moment, a master of temptation. This time, she placed her heated hands on my chest. I was instantly hard and she'd yet to go anywhere near my junk.

"You're a savvy guy, and I'm sure you can guess the end of the story," she said, slowly pressing the rest of her body against me. Her breasts felt like warm bread a few minutes out of the oven, even with our clothes still on. She must've known I was already fired up as she gently worked her groin against me. She leaned her forehead against mine and again, that foul yet sweet toxicity of her breath sent me into a deeper frenzy.

"You clocked the prick," I said, feeling shivers all over my body despite the hotness suddenly merging between us.

"Mmm hmm," Alexsandra confirmed, nudging her tongue out and dotting my lips with it. "Brained that son of bitch and watched his blood splatter on the bar counter along with the broken glass. I told the bastard it was for my father."

I remember stammering as Alexsandra wrapped her arms around me and pulled me snug against her, teasing my lips with hers. She purred as I took her into my arms in response. She sounded like I was tending a wound just by taking her into my embrace. As if Alexsandra hadn't been held in a very long time. A neglected cat finally finding a compassionate human hand sounds the same way.

"Wh-what did the guy do?"

"Hell if I know, Russ," she said with a wicked smile that should've scared me.

I laughed apprehensively instead of bailing like any rational person would do. This close to getting laid by a quasi-starlet, however, rationale went flying out the door.

"I ran the fuck right on out of there and never looked back," she said. "You have nice strong arms. Don't let me go."

Everything inside me was ignited and for a moment, my brain blitzed trying to process how any of this was happening. Alexsandra squeezed me tight, and my pecs wanted to gobble up her tits as she began massaging my shoulder blades. She looked out the window again and I did likewise, trying to stay patient when all I wanted to do then was get out of my clothes. A plane swooped down to the airport outside. There was a Union Jack on the tail fin.

"British Airways," we both muttered in sync and then we giggled like a couple of middle school kids in a cafeteria at the beginning of lunch.

"You want to come visit inside me," she said, not asked. She began a methodic grind that only fabric diminished. "I can tell how bad you do, Russ."

"Geez," I said, feeling idiotic. "I never expected *this* to happen, I..."

"Shut up," she said in a stronger voice, and she broke away one arm while continuing to rub my back. The free hand slinked slowly down the left side of my ribs, then she glided her fingertips along the top hem of my jeans until she reached my fly. "That story I told you is off-the-record. So is everything else from here on out until I say otherwise. Got it?"

"Definitely," I said, taking in a deep breath and sucking my stomach in to give Alexsandra the extra couple inches to undo me.

"Feel free to use my name, sometime, Russ," she whispered, unsnapping the button and lowering my zipper. "Although if you call me 'Alex,' I'll rip your dick off and send you on your way with it stuck in your ass. Good luck explaining *that* to the hospital."

"Sounds brutal, Alexsandra," I said with a nervous chuckle. "The Cannibal Corpse guys could take a few lessons from you."

"Who says they haven't?" she mocked with a wink.

As my jeans hit my ankles, she crashed her lips against mine and she seized my hand with a grip that hurt. Drawing me hard and close against her, she plunged my already greedy paw down the back of her sweats upon her bare ass. With nearly the same force as her grip, I seized her buttocks and kneaded ravenously.

Her bourbon-coated tongue darted all over mine and for a moment, I felt way out of my league.

"Relax, honey," she told me, parting away to lift her tank top up and over her head.

I was transfixed by all the tattoos that left mere inches of unblemished skin between them. The images were too much to take in, especially as I homed in on the silver bars piercing her ferocious nipples. I'd almost missed watching her sweatpants droop to the floor with an expert shimmy of her hips.

Alexsandra again smiled at me, obviously taking delight as I scanned her body, and then she turned her back to me, planted her hands on the windowsill and arched her rear end.

"Come watch the planes with me some more."

I remember shaking like I'd been left naked in a freezer as I complied.

"I can't make out the flag on the back of that one taking off now," Alexsandra said, still pointing her ass at me. It seemed like a hundred tattoos ran from the back of her neck down to her ankles. I nearly tripped as I rushed Alexsandra and probed myself between her legs.

"Well, hey there," she told me with a laugh, then a gasp as I slid myself into her.

As we ground each other tenderly at the wide-open window, I scoured the tattoos on Alexsandra's back and shoulders.

Egyptian hieroglyphics entwining a depiction of Horus appeared on her upper right shoulder. Beneath that was a powerful rendition of Anubis, holding his Ankh in the air with lightning beading upon the bottom tip.

On the opposite side of her back was The Toxic Avenger dribbling a smooshed ball of a guy like you see in the second film. Alexsandra also had a rogue's gallery of seventies and eighties horror moguls beneath Toxie, trailing straight down to her left buttock. Not the pedestrian Freddy Kruger, Jason Voorhees or Michael Myers. She had the zombified, naked form of Linnea Quigley's punkette "Trash" from *Return of the Living Dead* straddled overtop a snarling gargoyle yielding a dripping maw and next to them, the beefy goon Buddy from *Slaughterhouse.*

At the bottom of Alexsandra's spine, which was considered a "tramp stamp" in the tattooing world, sat the hideous Cape Cod from *The Amityville Horror* with a horde of demons dancing upon the roof. Overtop her left kidney was an extreme close-up of Sissy Spacek's Carrie White, training her vengeful glare upon the world after her pig blood dousing.

"Russ," Alexsandra muttered. "I can tell you haven't been laid in a while, so I'm holding back. I really like you, so I'm going to give you another secret. Not everyone I've been with knows this about me, so listen up. Are you able to go a few more minutes?"

"I think so," I mumbled, trying to keep my unhurried thrust going.

"I want you to go faster and don't you dare lose your load until I say."

"I'll do my best," I responded, feeling slightly perturbed by her officiousness, but I reminded myself I was having sex with Alexsandra Mundy of The Grit City Deviants, for crying out loud. She could be the boss all she wanted.

"I'm almost there," she said, pushing herself harder onto me. "Look at the hotel across the way. See him?"

"See what?" I asked, gasping as Alexsandra ground herself on me like she wanted to butt punch me across the room.

"The pervert with the binocs."

"Holy hell," I chortled.

"We're inviting people like him by doing it in front of a wide-open window, so let's give him a grand finale. When I tell you to, I want you to bite me on the slope of my right shoulder. Just like a vampire, but not on the carotid. Cool?"

"Say what?"

"It triggers an instant orgasm if the rhythm down there is fast enough. Now *fuck* me, Russ."

We went at it furiously as I tried not to laugh at the Toxic Avenger smirking back at me, his crushed human basketball looking gonzo. It took everything I had not to lose it.

"Bite me!" she commanded me, her voice sounding out-of-nowhere scary.

Without thinking, I chomped down where she wanted it and Alexsandra screamed, half in pain and half with something I hoped resembled pleasure. She constricted against me and shuddered as I couldn't hold it anymore. I snatched her right breast since there's nothing finer than a deal closing tit grab when you come. Alexsandra buckled her hips, trying to swallow me even deeper before burbling, "Air Suisse..." as another plane touched down in the distance.

"Jesus," I said, grabbing her waist and grunting like a gorilla stressed by a banana that refused to open as I drained myself. "That was unbelievable."

Then I roared in hilarity as Alexsandra lifted her middle finger up to the gawker in the hotel across ours.

"That was insane," she heaved, reaching behind and pulling my head down for a kiss. I caressed her boob some more, partially for show at our peeper and partially because I didn't want any of this to end.

After we detached from one another, Alexsandra swung around and hugged me once more, kissing me and heaving her exhalations into my face. Her breath stank even worse and still I loved it. I wanted her again, but after a few post copulations and extra kisses, Alexsandra let go of me and she swung the curtains shut before flopping backwards onto the bed.

"You may interview me now," she said. "Don't get dressed, though, and bring your camera. A towel too, please."

If the camera had been in the bedroom with us and in Alexsandra's possession, no doubt she would've snapped off a doofy shot of me standing there with my mouth agape and my bare body trembling.

I wobbled on buckling legs and shaking thighs back to the other end of the suite and nearly fell over trying to pick up my recorder, spiral notebook and camera bag off the couch. I swung into the bathroom and shivered as my bare feet hit the cold tiles. I didn't bother turning on the light as I spread my gear across the extensive sink basin. I then grabbed a towel from its hanging rack. Even with the bathroom light off, the white towel was still bright enough to find.

When I came back into the bedroom, Alexsandra was still undressed with her knees elevated and it was evident she was hiding her stomach. I never thought anything about that then, but I do now, given the fact she'd taken measures to hide something critical even while laying me.

"I'd say we're friends now, yes?" she asked me without letting me answer. She took the towel I brought, patted herself dry and left it jammed there. She'd made a point to drape a portion of the towel over her belly. "I've dropped a fortune in ink, and I like showing off my body, so take all the pictures you want, except for my navel. That's off-limits."

At this, Alexsandra rolled and flipped over onto her stomach, making a concerted effort to keep her abdomen shielded with the towel. I'd thought that was weird, but my confusion was short-lived in full admiration of the same view I'd had during sex, only now I saw an entire cosmos spilling down the backs of her legs. Alexsandra had countered the gory mayhem of her monster mash down her back with a much more soothing celestial map on those parts of her legs. Planets, meteors, comets, spiral galaxies. It was the universe revealed upon flesh.

"Start the recorder and ask your first question," she said in a slightly sluggish voice. "I trust I needn't remind you any snaps you take are confidential."

With my crusting and wilting penis joggling between my sweaty thighs, I pushed the record button on my Olympus VN-8000PC and placed it onto the nightstand next to the bed. Then I thumbed on my digital camera as I swung back to the foot of the bed.

"Why, Alexsandra?" I asked, lifting my lens after the camera bing-bonged to life. I zoomed in just enough to center her bottom within the frame and took the first shot. It should be noted a second pair of scaly hands reaching from the cosmos of her legs were engraved from her upper thighs into the bottom creases of her buttocks. I'd been so busy with the act at the window I'd missed taking inventory of those tattooed talons sinking into her glutes.

"Why *what?*" she moaned back.

"Why would you trust me? We've never met until today. Well, you reached out to me at Facebook first, which is unheard of."

"Russ, sweetie," she said, tilting her head so she wasn't as muffled by the pillows on her bed. "Don't overthink it, okay? It's just sex. Enjoy the moment and start the interview, already."

Again, I was slightly annoyed by her bossiness, but I panned out with my camera and got her full frame from head-to-toe. She seemed satisfied by this as she lurched back onto her knees and opened her legs so I could see more of where I'd been only moments ago. I noticed she'd left the towel flat on the bed, though I still couldn't quite detect what she had been covering. It became a moot point as the camera hungrily devoured her as I had moments ago.

"Um," I said, trying to remember one of my questions as Alexsandra rose to a full kneeling position with her back still to me. She crisscrossed her ankles in a way I'm frightened to say now I found adorable then. I kept firing off shots with the camera. She shook her clammy hair out and tilted her head back so I could catch a partial profile. Her eyes were closed but her mouth was titled upwards with apparent satisfaction.

"Anytime, now," she said, this time leaning further backwards so her breasts pushed into the air. Camera flashes looked like a strobe light as I took picture after picture.

"So," I mustered, shifting my position so I could snap her from another angle. Alexsandra soaked up the attention I was giving her with the camera, though now she started making the concentrated effort to keep one arm covered over her abdomen.

"Come on, Russ, I know I'm hot, but *focus*, will you? Sound check's in an hour fifteen and I need ten minutes of those to get to the venue."

Getting my thoughts into order despite the awkwardness of the moment, I said, "You can consider this off-the-record too, since you haven't said otherwise yet. How do you feel about these no-lifers who throw nasty insults at you on the metal chat boards? The ones who say you're only popular because of—"

"Because of my stunning body," Alexsandra finished for me, as she adjusted her position and splayed her legs outwards to give me a full-frontal view, minus the part she was blocking with her hands. If you look at the picture, she's plainly advertising her flower but trying her damnedest to block her stomach. "Well, let's go *on* record, since your recorder's running anyway."

"Works for me," I said, taking a few shots of just her face, then one arm sleeve of tattoos, then the other, then only her breasts. I tried to pan in upon her intersecting arms to see what I could get, but Alexsandra shook a forefinger at me with a forbidding expression, which I managed to take as well. When I look at that shot now, I get the quakes and not for any of the right reasons.

"Don't be naughty, Russ," she admonished me as she pulled her legs inward to once again cover her belly. I took at least thirteen shots of that position alone from multiple angles, shame on me. "As for the trolls, you're absolutely right. They have no lives. They're jealous of me and they're jealous of you."

"They'd be *really* jealous if they could see me now," I said dumbly.

"Fuckin' A right," Alexsandra agreed. "You and me, we're part of something they're not. Those limp dicks wish they were up onstage doing what I do. They wish they were on the road doing what you and I are doing right now. The reality of things, it isn't always like this. I haven't enjoyed any physical intimacy in weeks until now, and that's just the tolls of running the road trying to make money off merch sales and the slimming house takes. Not every venue's been sold-out. Tonight's not. For the record sales we had as a band when we started out, well, we get a fourth less of our royalties now, thanks to the dwindling music market. Don't get me wrong, I love what I do. I love performing and meeting our fans. When I'm onstage, it's such a rush. I know how much of a cliché that sounds, but there's nothing like raging for the fans from city-to-city, and *that* is what prompts the hatred from the cellar dwellers out there. I'm not trying to generalize, but metal fans are such douches. You know this."

I kept reeling off photos of Alexsandra as she dropped her knees and then began caressing the lower slopes of each breast with one hand, while keeping the other draped over her stomach.

She slipped up, though. She'd finally left enough open for me to spot one of the tattoos she'd been attempting to hide from me. I keep wondering if it had been purpose, given what I'd soon learn about Alexsandra Mundy. Had she been baiting me even further, beyond the sex?

Given Alexsandra's recently cut-short life, I can tell you my camera caught a hideous picture of a giant black widow spider gorging on the splayed innards of a man screaming in agony. Right where Candy Cassidy's groomed pubic hair stopped. I'm looking at the picture right now and I want to scream.

Back then, I nearly dropped my camera upon the tattoo's revelation and I'm positive my bumbling prompted Alexsandra's command to stop photographing her.

"What'd you take, an easy hundred pictures of me?" she quipped, rolling over again. "More than enough to get you through a few lonely nights."

"Right," I said, trying to compose myself as I shut off the camera, but that grisly image of the black widow chowing down on the howling guy changed everything. I was startled, naked, having fucked someone I suddenly suspected had committed murder at some point in her life.

Turns out, I wasn't wrong in that assumption.

I had to stay in the game, even though I was fearing for my life right then. "Um, next question, what is your most personal tattoo and what's the story behind it?"

"Hmm," Alexsandra moaned, squinting at me initially with what I detected to be suspicion. "I would say the one on my upper right arm here. The cherub you see there is my baby sister, Sabrina. She died from SIDS, so I never really knew her. Yet she was the sweetest thing, and her death certainly played hell in my parents' lives. I think half the reason my dad eventually hit the bottle so hard was guilt over losing my mom and the other half over losing Sabrina."

"At least once a day I try to imagine what Sabrina would've been like if she'd lived. Would she have been a dancer? A singer like me? An artist? God forbid, a fucking *accountant*? Sabrina never had a chance at life, so this way, I'm able to carry her with me wherever I go. Does that sound messed up?"

"No," I said, placing my camera onto the nightstand next to the recorder and trying to come up with another question by memory, even though my spiral was only a handful of steps away atop the bureau.

"Why don't you lay down with me for a few minutes?" Alexsandra invited as she shifted backwards into the pile of pillows, while hurriedly snagging and planting one of them over her midsection.

I left the recorder running and swung onto the bed. It was in Alexsandra's receptive arms that I laid my head. She drew my face onto her chest, and I felt unbelievably safe there. Scary when you understand the hidden truth about Alexsandra Mundy.

"Those claw mark tats," I said, loud enough for the recorder's benefit. "What's the deal there?"

"Well, Russ, I guess I'm just a bit of a horror freak. I love fright flicks, as I'm sure you could tell from my back, so I got a pretty good high one night before a show. Wichita, of all places. I sat with this greasy backwoods lancer, Dennis, who may have looked like a scag, but he's greatly skilled with a needle, as you can tell. He did Buddy on my back when we came through Wichita another time. Anyway, I paid a pretty penny for Buddy, but Dennis offered to do my tits for me at a much cheaper rate and well, you know, for a chance to run his crank through my cleavage before he got started. I can still smell his rotten funk on my neck, and that tattoo hurt like a bitch, not that I needed the pussyball, mind you. Hey, the artwork speaks for itself, right?"

I nearly pulled away from her with the mere implication that my face was resting in a spot where some hick had once left his non-inking mark, but then Alexsandra had me roll over, so my head landed in the pillow on her lap, and I was looking upwards at her.

We spent another twenty minutes on-the-record as Alexsandra stroked my hair while giving me a rock-solid interview I knew would be a laydown for *Thunder*. Afterwards, she told me she wanted me to get up and turn the tape recorder off. I could've fallen asleep in her lap, but after fulfilling her request, I turned around to find Alexsandra kneeling upwards on the bed again. The pillow was removed. So were her arms.

"If there's anything I consider off-the-record, Russ," she said, now in a stone-cold tone, "It's *this.*"

Alexsandra made a full circle around her tummy with her left hand, calling attention to skin art that has tormented me upon its revelation. Why I'd been the lucky one to bear witness to them, I'll never know.

From her belly button down to her shaven pussy was far more than the chomping black widow I'd caught earlier. I now saw a slew of gory depictions of butchered men. I saw knives plunged into skulls. I saw beheaded corpses with spurting arteries. I saw atrocity after atrocity inked onto Alexsandra Mundy and I was suddenly mortified.

"You've probably read about several murders in the Midwest panhandle attributed to a woman the press calls 'The Widow.' Sound familiar?"

"Uhh—" I said with a suddenly repulsed feeling in my stomach.

The Widow.

Yes, *of course* I knew about The Widow. Everyone in proximity to the slayings or within reach of the internet knew about them. Thus far, eight male victims had been attributed to The Widow, who remained at large. Two had been beheaded and positioned upright on the side of the road on Interstate 70 in Kansas using props to upend the bodies. Their heads were found directly across the street, staring back at their decapitated corpses. The internet sickos had made the story viral, and the FCC had a hell of a time getting pirated photos pulled from the web. Every time the pictures seemed to be gone, someone else took up the cause and reposted them on junk blogs that were almost always torn down a week later. Rumor has it, those pictures have found a place of prominence and permanence on the dark web at a members-only site called "The Widow's Work Lives On."

Alexsandra said nothing else for nearly a minute as she surveyed my reaction with curiosity. Then she showed me a sickening grin I wanted to run away from, as she pointed at herself and tapped her sternum, right between the bloody claw marks.

"Oh, f-fuck," I stuttered.

"Russ, I don't want to lose you as a friend," she told me, tilting her head to the side and continuing to scan me studiously.

"What the hell?" I blurted, unaware I was backing away from the bed and Alexsandra.

"Don't be afraid," she told me, training her stare back at me with a shivery expression cast upon her writhing countenance. "These tattoos are what you think they are. I *am* The Widow, but you can rest assured, you won't be one of *them*. So long as you don't dick me over. The only other people who've seen these tattoos aren't—well, they're not around to testify to them, let's just say that. They've become a part of my collection, you get it?"

"Y-yeah," I answered, freezing in place, still naked and now far away from my camera and recorder at this point.

"Lookee here," Alexsandra said, her crimson-streaked eyes flashing wide as she pointed to a gruesome tattoo showing the blunt end of a hammer crunching into a bearded man's skull. The details were so alarming they attested to the artist and ultimately the victim. "That's Dennis. Can you imagine? The moron agreed to ink it before I—you know."

As abruptly heated as she'd become, Alexsandra settled back down, her eyes easing, her shoulders going slack. I don't think she was ever aware of it, but she burped. Another time, I would've laughed.

"I'm going to take a shower now," she said. "I'd prefer it if you joined me, but I'll understand if you don't. You *will* wait for me before leaving, regardless. I know how to get to you, since Frannie gave me your particulars so I could validate your credentials. The choice is yours, take a shower with me or sit on the bed until I'm done. Either way, I don't want to wake up Gus, and I need a ride into town, so you'll repay me the favor I just gave you."

I'd understand wholeheartedly if you're unable to believe me at this point, but as Alexsandra slithered off the bed and gave me a pat on the ass and a gentle pull on my dirty, flaccid manhood, I followed her to the shower, more for the sake of self-preservation.

Under the hot water, she kissed me and pressed herself all over me, but I couldn't reciprocate this time. I was scared shitless now and feeling immobilized. Alexsandra tried to get me fired up a second time, but the cylinders were dead; more accurately, they were stymied. When I couldn't get it up and stood there trembling in the shower, Alexsandra took the bar of hotel soap and she washed me with it, then herself. She said not a word while doing it. If she'd been mad I was so frightened, she never showed it. Instead, she kissed me one more time before leaving me there in the shower. I stood there, stupefied, for another five minutes.

"It's been a genuine afternoon delight," Alexsandra called to me as I stood in shock under the shower nozzle, the water growing cold the longer I stayed there. "But as I said, I have sound check, and that's now in half an hour, so let's get a move on. You're staying for the show, right?"

"Sure," I said, just barely over the hiss of the shower, now shooting trails of icy water at me.

We drove in silence into the midtown section of Philadelphia, swinging through Chinatown and hooking right onto Arch Street. At her insistence, I put on The Circle Jerks' *Wild in the Streets* that I had sitting in my CD carrier. She bobbed and thrashed her head during the ride. Me, I'm not sure I'll ever be able to listen to that album ever again.

"God, I love Chinese grub," she said to me as I pulled to a stop in front of the Easy Ride Club. "I'd like to see you again, Russ. Maybe you wanna grab a bite after sound check? You're welcome to come and sit in on rehearsal if you like."

"I got work early in the morning," I said, trying not to upset her. "I was going to hang for the show, but I think I'm gonna drive back and get some sleep. Some other time, maybe."

"I see," Alexsandra told me in a stale voice. "I've put you through a lot today, I get it. Here, I want you to have this, so wherever we're playing, you have standing VIP."

From the inside of her leather jacket, Alexsandra pulled out an all-access laminate badge. I'd been given tons of them in the past, but I keep wondering now if the true crime geeks out there wouldn't pay top dollar for a VIP pass issued by The Widow herself. I'm holding it in my hand right now as I recount this, considering The Widow's untimely death yesterday.

Alexsandra kissed me once more, pushing her lips hard onto mine. I tried to give as good as I got from her, just to keep her from wanting to hunt me down now that she'd given me all her secrets. I even grabbed her right breast, just to make a show of it. Like earlier, she purred at me as I thumbed over the pierced nipple bar beneath her Hank, III t-shirt before she removed my hand and placed it gently on top of the gear shift between our hips. She patted my hand a couple times, then laced her fingers into mine and squeezed them tight before dislodging them altogether.

"Don't you *ever* turn into a fake friend, Russ," Alexsandra said with a playful warning I still took deadly serious as she got out of my car. "The repercussions wouldn't be pleasant."

She blew me a kiss from outside and slammed my car door before bouncing into the club.

I drove home from Philly with no music on the entire ride.

Yesterday, all the music and counterculture sites lit up with breaking news.

Alexsandra Mundy had been found dead backstage at a rock club in Columbus, Ohio called The Embers. She'd mixed opioids with an entire fifth of whiskey, one-ups of how Prince and long-ago AC/DC singer, Bon Scott checked out of their respective rock 'n roll damnations. All she'd divulged to me, Alexsandra never confided she'd been in physical pain as to rely on opioids. In my hour-plus with her, I'd learned she was addicted to pain as much as drinking and killing. All of it, with the opioids, being her undoing.

The metal world is in mourning, and I would be too, had Alexsandra not shown me the evil that lay beneath, so to speak. All I know is The Widow is at rest and I'm not sure whether I should come clean with all I was given.

I only captured a sliver of the spider tattoo, but who's to say if it's legit material evidence or merely circumstantial. What the coroner might think upon examination of those awful abdomen tats, I shudder to dwell upon. It's his burden now, though I doubt he or the investigators will put two and two together Alexsandra Mundy was The Widow. Makes me wonder if Alexsandra, as a mid-30s murderess, thought ahead about her own funerary plans and whether she'll be buried or cremated. Material evidence potentially going up in flames.

All I know is I'm more afraid of the repercussions with Alexsandra dead than alive.

I've considered deleting those nude photos thousands of times in the short time I've had them, but I can't, mortified by them as I am now. I damn well should, but I keep clicking and gawking at them anyway, first to last, like a slide show. I'm doing it right now. I mean, shit, I'd shagged The Widow and lived to talk about it. How am I supposed to convey *that* under oath in court testimony?

There's Nuke Girl, hitting my instant messenger, confirming our lunch date in Manhattan next week.

Yes, we're on, Jenny.

Now she's asking if I know about Alexsandra Mundy.

Yes, Jenny, and *then some*.

Meteor Shit

Kevin Plympton descended the school bus and paused on the last step, scanning with trepidation hovering over him for the three weeks since seventh grade began. Both of his flimsy arms were throbbing from multiple punches he'd absorbed in the hallways all day long. He'd checked himself in the boys' room after hiding in the stall and waiting for everyone to clear and counted the fresh bruises. All eight of them. He'd been late for Math II because of it.

"Go on, kid," Kevin heard behind him, a deep baritone voice reminding him of Darth Vader, only without the refined gentleman's polish and the echo effect sounding like it was being done inside a bucket. This was more of an everyday man's gruff sent to him. From the fat, coffee-skinned bus driver who was playing songs on a transistor radio hanging over his steering wheel. Right now, Earth, Wind and Fire was ba-de-yaaaaing their way through a happier September than Kevin was having thus far.

"Okay," Kevin sent back to the driver, swinging his head over his shoulder to see the guy slowly bobbing his head in time to the up-tempo soul music Kevin would've appreciated more from the safety of his own home.

"In this lifetime, if you don't mind, young man," the driver said in his nicer-than-Vader retort, but the impatience in his voice was plenty clear. The driver shook his head in pity down at Kevin, because he knew, like everyone huddled at the bus stop instead of heading for their houses knew.

Something was going down.

And Kevin was the star attraction.

With a sigh through his teeth, a squeeze inside his bladder that would've released into his muddy brown corduroy pants had Kevin not taken a whiz at school day's end, he got off the bus.

The wheeze-hiss of the closing door behind him and the slow, loud acceleration of the bus pulling away rang of sealed fate. Of predestined doom.

Because there was Scott Schneider.

An innocent enough name, like that guy *Dwayne* Schneider, the superintendent on *One Day at a Time,* who was kind of a schmuck, but a likeable schmuck who'd been winning over the Romano family one *week* at a time on the tube. Everybody liked Schneider, including the smart alecky and insanely hot Barbara, her mouthy rebel of a sister Julie and their redhead-bobbed mom, Ann. Everybody in the viewership liked Schnider too, it seemed.

There was nothing innocent nor charming about Scott Schneider, except maybe to his friends, who seemed to worship the very ground he walked on—more like spat upon, as if his brackish saliva was disobedient divinity itself.

"What's up, cock face?"

Kevin ground his teeth beneath his dry lips so he wouldn't give Scott or any of the others the satisfaction of knowing how hurt he felt, how angry he was. He carried a raging fire encased by his slight chest currently covered by a filmy baseball shirt decked with the print of the two angels dragging on their elysian cigarettes on Black Sabbath's *Heaven and Hell* album. The iron-on decal was beginning to show cracking and wear. It was a shirt Kevin slept in as much as he wore around school, and it was starting to show signs of overuse. Of wilting. Of coming to an end of its usefulness.

Which is how Kevin felt, blowing an oleaginous strand of his grubby brown strands off his brow.

"When's the last time you washed your hair, Kevin?" Marcia LaCroix taunted him from behind a pair of wide-framed spectacles nearly as frog-eyed big as safety goggles. Her gungy spread of black hair was dumped across the shoulders of a mauve colored zipper sweat jacket with twin white piping down the back of each sleeve. Having the gumption to cast stones, Marcia was wearing a cottony Strawberry Shortcake shirt that looked more like the top of a pajama set.

Kevin had his Trapper Keeper, two of his textbooks and a paperback copy of Stephen King's *Cujo* locked against his hip. *Cujo* was the story of a loveable Saint Bernard who turned rabid, trapping an unfaithful mom and her son inside her broken-down Pinto on the very farm she'd taken the car to for mechanical help. Plot-twist, said farmer-mechanic had left for vacation and there was no way to get off the premises without testing her luck against a diseased dog playing cat-and-mouse (the dog variation, anyway) with said mother and son unable to escape her dead wheels in the dead summer heat. Three fourths of the way through, a lot of death for a small cast of characters.

"I'm *talking* to you, rim job!" Scott Schneider bellowed at Kevin, who took his first hopeful steps away from the gathering, knowing it was futile. Scott's latest jibe had struck the funny bone of the other middle schoolers, nine aside from Scott and his closest crony, Eric Jackson. They all guffawed like those laugh tracks on t.v. sitcoms. Raised up in tandem, then settled to immediate quiet. Like they needed prompting to give flatlining jokes some sense of lilt. "I asked you what's up."

"Nothing," Kevin answered Scott, shooting his most hated enemy all the malice he had from behind his brown eyes. Knowing he wasn't going to act on his pervading thoughts of fighting back for once. Thus far, Scott hadn't hit him, tripped him up or kicked him from behind the knees as Schneider loved to do. Thus far.

"How does a nerd like you like something badass like Black Sabbath?" Scott sneered, reaching for Kevin's shirt, apparently to tug on it for emphasis. He himself was wearing a green and yellow striped Izod, but Scott was more roughneck than preppie, considering he was already smoking Camels at age 13.

Kevin gave no response as Scott rattled on, knowing he had an audience eating up his every maneuver. They might clap even if he picked his nose in front of them.

"You wear that shirt all the fucking time it's beginning to smell. You do your laundry, right? Or at least give it to your Ma to wash? Or what is it, your family's so poor you have nothing else to wear? Shit, that must be it, Plympton, 'cuz I doubt you can name one goddamn song from *Heaven and Hell*. Tell you what, you name me one song that's not the title track, you can be on your merry way."

"'Die Young,'" Kevin blurted, not so much with excitement but with internal satisfaction. He'd played the cassette of *Heaven and Hell* so often in his bedroom he knew the entire album in sequential order. Accordingly, he began reciting the first three tracks of the album. "'Neon Knights,' 'Children of the Sea,' 'Lady Evil.' That's half the album right there."

Scott appeared miffed. Embarrassed, maybe. "Okay, smartass," he gnashed. "You know your *Heaven and Hell*. Now go fuck yourself."

For one optimistic moment, Kevin thought Scott was going to honor their agreement. For a second encouraging instant, Kevin slid past Scott and Eric Johnson. Even the other kids made way for him to pass by.

He should've known better.

Kevin only got a few steps away from the bus stop when he felt something like a mule kick him from behind, targeting the books wedged at his hip. His hip sang a song of pain with the same baleful swoon as Ronnie James Dio did for Black Sabbath on "Lonely is the Word."

The Trapper Keeper jettisoned from Kevin's grip, fanning open and vomiting a score of ditto sheets and pulled free looseleaf papers, sending them cascading everywhere to the ground. The textbooks, English Literature and Science II, hit the pavement, spread out with immediately creased pages.

"The fuck is this shit?" Kevin heard from behind, knowing without seeing it Scott had his copy of Stephen King's *Cujo* in his possession. "What the hell is a 'Cujo?' I mean, that sounds like the sneeze of a retard or something. Am I right, Eric? Ah-ah-ah-CUJO!!!"

"Bless you," Eric cracked in a deadpan manner, following that with an ugly snort-laugh sounding more like a phlegm hock. "What kinda weird shit are you into, Plympton?"

"Give it back," Kevin said in a low voice as he hurriedly gathered his loose papers into his Trapper Keeper.

"What was that, fuck nuts?" Scott growled to Kevin's back. "You want this back, is that what I'm hearing?"

Having crammed everything back into the Trapper Keeper where Kevin would reassemble it all later, he turned to Scott, who was already within arm's length.

"Yeah," Kevin whispered, trying to muster something louder, stronger, more authoritative. His speech got caught up inside a quivering chest which wanted to see Scott Schneider's head suddenly explode into the most riotous shower of crimson gore. Like that guy in the *Scanners* movie Kevin watched three times on HBO over the summer break.

"Oh, you want your 'Cujo' book, I see," Scott said, making a show of it by holding the Stephen King book high over his head and waving it for the onlookers to see. As jocks did with their championship trophies.

"It's a horror novel," interjected Katie Baier from the top of a flimsy yellow windbreaker she didn't really need on a 72-degree early fall day. "I read it. It's awesome. I—"

"Shut up, Katie!" Scott shouted at her. "Nobody's talking to you. You, Plympton. You want your book back? Then kiss my ass."

"What?" Kevin winced, pulling away from Scott with a repulsion on his face matched by many of the other kids. Katie Baier had already retreated down the sidewalk for her house.

"You heard me," Scott taunted, swiveling his Wrangler-covered hip to show a fading patch at his rear end amidst the deeper blue denim surrounding it. "Kiss my ass, right here in front of everyone. Then kiss Eric's. After that, you can have your book back."

"I'll pass on that shit," Eric groaned, throwing out a double wave of no-go.

"Fine, whatever. Get on your knees and kiss it, Plympton."

Still holding the *Cujo* novel, Scott bent his butt straight in Kevin's direction and looking around him to see what reception he got.

He'd gone too far this time, because nobody was egging Scott on. Two other kids, Michael Tan and his one-year-younger sister, Jeanna, rolled out on the nasty scene.

"No," Kevin said, for the first time feeling a rise in his gorge that wasn't bile, as happened to him often after eating half a bag of barbecue chips with two cans of 7-Up. It was shock blended with anger, and it flooded his body. His heartbeat skipped out of rhythm before spiking with such ferocity it felt like it might detonate. His eyes pulsed inside their sockets, like they might blast out of each pupil like that poor schmuck, Rick, who had his head crushed from both sides by the hockey masked killer, Jason Voorhees in *Friday the 13th Part III.*

"The hell you say?" Scott fumed, leaping in midair to turn himself before swinging the book sticking out from his right hand and popping Kevin upside the left cheek.

His insurrection quashed as fast as it had risen, Kevin staggered on his feet from the blow, but he didn't go down.

"Heaven and Hell, I can tell," Scott Schneider mocked Kevin, throwing the novel at his chest, which bounced off him and hit the ground, pushing the pages helter skelter and instantly creasing the spine of the paperback which Kevin had taken great lengths to gently preserve. "Fool, fool, motherfucker."

***

Kevin's parents were still another hour arriving home from work.

Normally his after school routine was to flop in front of the television and kick on MTV music videos while reading the latest *Fangoria* magazine or *Justice League of America* comics. He scored these from a local High's convenience store when his parents took him along for their frequent hikes to get two-liter sodas and cigarettes.

Today, however, Kevin was mad.

Madder than mad.

His aching, beaten with a Stephen King paperback head was stuffed with violent thoughts of a bloodbath. Specifically, Scott Schneider's blood.

The kind of thoughts Kevin could only confess and release to his Philips tape recorder only when he had the house to himself.

He tore open a fresh pack of Certron 60-minute cassette tapes, which Kevin usually used to record songs he liked off 98 Rock, which played heavier, louder music than the Baltimore pop station, B-104. He'd ditched the latter the moment he came across Rush's "Limelight" dialing around the radio channels on the family stereo. Instant love, those throbbing bass lines, razor sharp guitar pickups and the best drumming he'd ever heard in his young life. Tom and snare rolls seducing him to an entirely new, innovative way to rock.

Kevin then recorded other songs by the Canadian prog rock trio, along with hard grinding tunes from AC/DC, Van Halen, Lynyrd Skynyrd, Triumph, Kiss, Quiet Riot and Def Leppard before graduating to the *real* heavy stuff like Iron Maiden, Judas Priest, Saxon and of course, Kevin's favorite band, Black Sabbath. He captured all these songs by placing the Philips recorder next to the radio and staying immaculately silent as he taped each song. Only once had his mother barged into his room with a summons for dinner, ruining his recording of Accept's bold and bawdy "Balls to the Wall" on 98 Rock. It had taken nearly the rest of the week to catch the song again and get a clear transfer.

In the case of Black Sabbath, Kevin had collected most of the band's catalog on cassette tape, the Ozzy Osbourne years and the Ronnie James Dio years. His favorite Sabbath albums were *Master of Reality*, *Sabotage*, *Mob Rules* and, of course, *Heaven and Hell*. The band had recently released a new album, *Born Again*, with their third different singer, Ian Gillan, who'd transplanted himself from Deep Purple.

Despite the scary demon baby yowling on the cover of *Born Again,* Kevin's mother had bought him the tape a week ago after its release on September 8th. After two full listens, Kevin was still trying to warm up to it.

Times filled with conflict and fury like this, Kevin liked to use the Philips recorder to sound off and listen to his angry thoughts, usually taping over them after hitting a few playbacks.

"I want him dead," Kevin growled, his chin waggling over the perforated square serving as the tape recorder's microphone. "Dead. DEAD! I wanna fucking kill Scott Schneider! I want to tear his head off and kick it around like a soccer ball! I wanna roll it to some stray dog and see if the mutt'll piss all over it! Kill the son of a bitch! Kill him! Pull Schneider's guts out and shove them back down his throat! Die, already, you piece of shit! DIE!!!"

The tears swelled in Kevin's eyes then released. The tape recorder caught his sobbing, not that Kevin cared.

"Why do they all hate me so much?!?" he shrieked into the microphone. "What the hell did I do to any of those bastards! I can't change classes without someone punching me. *Girls,* even! What did I even do? I can't go to the bathroom without someone trying to jump me, without someone banging on the stalls, or throwing milk cartons over the partition at me, still filled! The shit gets all over me and I stink the rest of the day! Jesus Christ, I don't bother anyone, so why? WHY?!?

He paused, watching the double spindles on the Philips machine twirl in calm revolutions, taping the abrupt silence.

Kevin felt a rising inside his chest, boiling bile which he managed to swallow back down after it burned his throat. Intestinal gas took its place. In a hurry, Kevin planted his mouth directly over the microphone and recorded a long, liquidy belch.

Laughing behind what he considered a champion ralph, Kevin added, "I don't pray much, God, and Ma doesn't go for the Old Testament wrath and vengeance stuff. New Testament's her thing, and I'm blathering, sorry, God. You see me down here. You see what they're doing to me. I fucking hate them all! Sorry again, Lord, I didn't mean to cuss in the middle of a prayer. All I ask from you, and I'll do whatever you want of me from here on out in my crappy life, is to find a way to get rid of Scott Schneider. Permanently."

Kevin shut the recorder off then rewound it to the beginning. Pressing the play button, he listened to his tirade as he scoured his bedroom walls filled with cut-out pictures from *Fangoria*. Lodged to the walls with a mix of silver, yellow, blue and red colored thumbtacks. A black-and-white picture of Michael Myers stalking Jamie Lee Curtis in a hospital corridor from *Halloween II*. A grotesque photo of the demonized Linda Blair from the original *Exorcist,* her face covered with gashes and green barf. A full-page advertisement for Stephen King and George A. Romero's tribute to 1950s horror comics, *Creepshow.*

The same splash treatment for John Carpenter's bloody remake of *The Thing,* the latter being the most fun Kevin had ever had in his living room. His parents had let him watch it after previewing it ahead of time. Such glorious splatter and gut churning viscera thrilled Kevin upon first contact. He still hadn't decided what was fouler, the guy whose lopped off head sprouted alien spider legs and crawled off, or the Norwegian guy Kurt Russell and company found in a shelled-out science station in Antarctica. That poor fool looked like one side of his face had been stepped on by something triple his weight.

The only non-horror item pinned to Kevin's wall was a corner page advertisement featuring Sylvester Stallone, hefting a semiautomatic colossus in his brawny grip as Vietnam Veteran John Rambo in *First Blood,* cut out from *The Baltimore Sun's* movie listings.

"They drew first blood," Kevin muttered in homage of Rambo's edict over the walkie talkie to his former commanding officer, Colonel Trautman.

Laughing one more time at his guttural belching, Kevin rewound his tape a fourth time, then plunged his fingers down over the record and play buttons simultaneously. He stared down at the Philips recorder blankly, letting the machine capture only his silent rage.

***

The next day was Saturday, Kevin's favorite day of the week. Not just because there was no school, but because Saturdays meant *Ghost Host* at 11:30 p.m. after the local news report and a *Get Smart* rerun on Channel 45.

Ghost Host Theatre was Kevin's weekly fix of old-time horror, all monochrome films from the Universal monster era through the atomic age B pictures of the 1950s, which he loved as much as the new movies. Movies featuring next to no blood and were sometimes as corny as the Ghost Host himself, a ghoulish creep of a man prowling into a basement laboratory with an overdubbed sinister drone making him sound like he could use a throat lozenge. On commercial breaks, the *Ghost Host* skulked back and forth inside a cheesy mock cemetery as he chatted up the week's spook selection with anecdotes about the lead actors and behind-the-scenes trivia Kevin was as fascinated with as the black-and-white movies themselves. The Ghost Host was played by George Lewis, who, funny enough, doubled as beloved daytime cartoon compere, Captain Chesapeake on the same channel.

This week was *The Tingler* from 1959 and starring Vincent Price, Kevin's all-time favorite horror actor. It would be the third time Kevin would see it and no doubt, his father would reminisce, as he did the last two times *The Tingler* was shown on *Ghost Host*, about the notorious novelty seat buzzers that were rigged in the theaters during its theatrical run. A gimmick which had delighted his dad as a teenager yet sent a few people screaming out of the theater back in the day. Kevin was so jealous.

Ghost Host was hours away and Kevin found himself in the shower after watching a gamut of Saturday morning cartoons featuring *The Charlie Brown and Snoopy Show, The New Scooby and Scrappy Doo Show, Dungeons and Dragons* and the dopey Mr. T animated series.

A bunch of dumb kid crap Kevin couldn't seem to purge out of his habits no matter how much horror movies and heavy music had been, of late, consuming his life.

He doused his hair with his mother's Strawberry Herbal Essence shampoo and stood there under the spritzing water, as hot as he could stand it. His skin had turned salmon pink then outright red from the scalding shower.

Kevin lost track of time, not that he was in any hurry. Marcia LaCroix's condemnation of his oily hair had left its impact on him, and he thought about her snide remark repeatedly. When he wasn't thinking about Scott Schneider cuffing him with his own book.

Kevin put his *Heaven and Hell* shirt into the hallway hamper, for a moment feeling like he was permanently letting it go altogether. He pacified himself by playing the first side of *Born Again* as he ruffled his wet hair with his towel, which also went into the hamper. He then chose a Baltimore Colts sweatshirt he hadn't worn in nearly a year. Save for a minute exposure of his belly, it surprisingly still fit him well.

His breath tasted of the pepperoni pizza they'd had the night before, which Kevin made a note to brush his teeth once the fifth track on side A of *Born Again,* the 7:35 "Zero the Hero" was finished. And it took forever to finish.

"This kinda sucks," he muttered in dismissal of the music, not that he would tell his mother. You didn't get cool parents who let their early-teen sons watch buckets of blood films (on the condition Kevin hide his face with a pillow during the nude scenes) and buy cassettes plastered by the spawn of Satan.

"Even I think Black Sabbath's hit a rut hearing that dreck," Kevin's dad said to him as he returned to the bathroom. He hadn't seen his father, thus Kevin jumped out of his skin upon hearing him. He was partially annoyed but mostly smiling inside, since there was very little which scared him in horror movies.

Real world terrors like Scott Schneider, a different story.

"Geez, man!" Kevin pretend scoffed at his dad.

"How about listening to some real music?" his dad joked, swinging for the stairwell. "Big Bopper, Danny and the Juniors, The Crests, now *that's* music. On a serious note, why don't you go outside for a bit? Take advantage of the Indian summer before the temperatures plummet and lock us indoors every weekend."

"Sure," Kevin replied, squeezing a generous portion of Crest onto his toothbrush, one that hadn't been used since Wednesday. Even he had to bemoan his own reflection in the vanity mirror which was just clearing of the imprinted steam. "No wonder they can't stand you, loser."

***

To the west of the Belmont townhome community was a spread of woods not much longer for this world, given the adjacent bulldozed mounds of dirt, two pushed as high as three stories. Signals of future development and subdivision on the horizon. The light timber, hardly valuable enough for construction repurpose, would be heading for an obtuse mulcher. Those creatures which called these woods their home would be forced into relocation.

One could simply walk around the dirt mounds, but that was no fun. Despite his freshening up, Kevin couldn't resist climbing up the side of the tallest mound in front of him. He'd done so frequently, and he saw the scores of indentations from his prior climbs. It took a small trot at the basin and a hop to get his footing, and Kevin was at the pointed summit in no time. Already his hands, Levis, Colts sweatshirt and white Nikes with the blue swooshes were grubby.

He took a deep breath at the top, surveying the rows of townhomes from Streaker Court and Middleton Street to the rear of his own Glazer Court. The shapes were universal, the same rear window scheme flushing from two at the top for their corresponding rooms to a widely spread casement in the kitchen. Some of the townhomes on his block had fenced-in back yards and others, like his own, had an open patch of land which took his father an easy five minutes to mow. From his vantage, Kevin could see the pulled over drapery blocking the view into his family's clubbed in basement.

Without a second thought, Kevin looked down in front of him, a steep slope dropping to an entry path into the woods. The first time he'd taken this mountain of dirt, stones and rocks, Kevin crashed halfway down the descent and cut up his right palm. The scar was still there. However, he'd gotten less clumsy and surer of himself. Kevin galloped down now, heels sinking into the dry earth to the point he could already hear his mother halting him at the front door to make him clap his sneakers before coming inside.

"I wish I was this brave with Schneider," he said to no one as he finished his succession, the closest specimen of life being a swooping starling hardly able to interpret his human babble.

Nearly every time Kevin came to the woods, he had them all to himself. There was only the time he'd come across a Hispanic family he figured lived in the Dutrow Apartments on the opposite end of the mini forest. They'd been splashing and laughing at the creek which slashed through the small ecosystem.

Immediately engulfed by fir trees, pines, hemlocks and birches, Kevin exhaled with a satisfied grin, same as he always did coming here. Truth be told, he loved being in the woods far more than his own bedroom. It was the pristine air, the rich smell of terpenes from the pine needles which often tickled his nostrils and made him sneeze from time-to-time. Also, the wildlife, whom he considered his muted friends: squirrels, chipmunks, jackrabbits and the occasional deer which greeted him cautiously, always from a distance.

The pine scent he loved suddenly turned sour. He'd smelled something like it before in the chemistry lab at school. Nasty business, enough to trigger nausea. Kevin thought he'd heard the chem teacher, Miss Covington, call it "sulfur."

"Ewww, what the—" he groaned, stopping in place and pinching his nostrils.

Maybe it was blood, as if one animal had killed another, for food, perhaps, and its gored remains were nearby. That would explain it.

A warning bell inside Kevin clanged, telling him it might be prudent to back out this time, to turn around and leave the woods.

Danger was afoot, it told him, and yet Kevin was compelled to go further, to find the source of the stench, since it was growing stronger the deeper he ventured.

"What *is* that?" he asked aloud, as if some benevolence of the woods might answer him.

His soiled sneakers scuffed the gritty trail. He punted pebbles without seeing how he was doing so. Only when a sizeable rock launched ahead of him and *tink-a-clinked* against other rocks did it occur to Kevin to pick up his feet as he went on.

For the second time today, Kevin was startled, frozen in his tracks, as a robin, of all things, rocketed past his right ear, pulling up to the skyline of the trees before swooping back down. The bird flapped its wings in suspension mere feet away from Kevin's face. Screeching and fluttering for a few seconds before dashing away.

"Jesus," Kevin whispered, sensing the robin's appearance for what it might've been. Balking at the incredible stink. Or worse, notification of an immediate threat.

Yet the odor had grown stronger and Kevin's curiosity right along with it. The last time he'd been this enquiring was when his mother was frying bacon and using a mesh splatter screen to cover the hissing and popping. When she'd stepped out of the kitchen, Kevin, despite knowing it was a positively dumb thing to do, pulled the screen away and leaned down into the sizzling pan. Only to have hot grease crack beneath him and douse his left cheek. A second glob had shot right into the same side eye. He'd spent the next ten minutes with a cool dishrag over the eye, his mother trying not to laugh at his blunder.

Here was the same thing, that unstoppable need to know, despite the hint of negative consequence.

It smelled even worse now, to the point Kevin knew he was within reach of the source.

Sure enough, he spotted a vapor trail, more like rolling fog keeping a low berth on the ground. Like those old vampire and werewolf movies on *Ghost Host,* silly looking clouds from an offscreen fog machine.

The only thing, this was real, and it was far from silly.

To his left, Kevin saw several trees which had been split apart, the bark scorched and ashy. Like a lumberjack came along and did a half ass job before outright giving up on the task. Carelessly tossing an unextinguished cigarette into the folds, to make matters worse.

"Whoa," he said, following the separation and busting up of the trees to find a gaping hole in the earth.

A gaping hole glowing a mustard yellow and smoldering like those German incense smokers Kevin's mother liked to burn every Christmas. One being a baker making Christmas cookies, his sack of piecemeal listed as "MEHL," the other being a gaping-mouthed Santa Claus. Jerks like Scott Schneider would no doubt have something derogatory to say about that.

The earth had been pulverized where the yellow emissions spewed. As if a couple of grave diggers had opened the ground up to drop three caskets inside instead of one. The crevice looked like an extraterrestrial mouth yowling from the land. No phone home, in this case. The damage had been done and there it would stay until it cooled off and Nature's defenses put it down for good.

No sign of that happening anytime soon as Kevin drew nearer to the cloudy fissure. Lord, did it stink!

The reek slammed into Kevin's nostrils, and despite his wanting to puke from the intrusion, he was committed now.

He spotted what appeared to be sectioned halves of a craggy orb, a bisected rock unlike anything he'd ever seen, save maybe for that meteor on display in the geology hall at the Smithsonian Museum of Natural History in Washington, D.C.

That's what this was, he was sure of it now. A meteor! Only a fast-plummeting meteor could do the damage he saw in front of him, even if Kevin thought the world had been spared, just a little, considering the gravitational pull should have turned this event into a full cataclysm.

The sallow muck pooling inside the space-made ditch was bubbling, like a pot of potatoes, which he knew was on the menu for dinner tonight along with pork chops and succotash. His mother would use that Shake 'n Bake seasoning Kevin loved so much.

Dinner didn't matter, not now, if at all. Neither would *The Tingler* later tonight. How could Kevin concentrate on make-believe terror when he had the real thing before him now?

Buhhh-loop! Kevin heard coming from the fractured earth. *Buhhh-loop! Buhhh-loop!*

For whatever reason, out of the same weird cosmos the meteor came from perhaps, Kevin conjured that old ditty about witches' work above a cauldron. And this was a cauldron of sorts, wasn't it?

"Bubble, bubble, toil and trouble," Kevin moaned, feeling stupid for doing so.

Buhhh-loop! it went on. Like a slow heating soup. Like a bathtub fart.

Finally, it dawned on Kevin what the interstellar goo was. Stephen King had nailed it to the sheets, playing his own lunkhead creation, Jordy Verrill, in *Creepshow,* faced with the same extraordinary experience as Kevin.

"Meteor shit," Kevin said with a heave. "That's exactly what this is. Meteor shit."

Unlike Jordy Verrill's poor misfortune of being assimilated by mutated fauna after trying to cash in on his galactic find of the century, Kevin would do no such thing. In fact, the longer he laid eyes upon the haze, the shorter breaths he took to contend with the smell, he began to spot something beneath the rolling gases.

More than something.

A *whole lot* of something.

"Oh, my God," he whispered to find strews of bones. Tiny bones, not human, some of them separated and scattered like the broken off twigs that were part and parcel to any wooded environment.

Some of the bones were still intact to pearl colored rib cages, limbs and pelvises. Devoid of skin, feathers and hair.

Animal bones.

A pause in the emissions, as if on purpose and with the intent of scaring the absolute hell out of Kevin, confirmed it to be true. He now saw small skulls, eaten down to the raw finish of their skeletal matter. What he assumed belonged to the same squirrels, bunnies and birds he saw on a routine basis in the woods.

Upon this revelation, the smoke thickened yet again, hiding the evidence as it were.

"Did you do that on purpose?" he asked, spotting a chipmunk nosing around the huffing perimeter of the meteor impact site. Like Kevin, yielding to wonder instead of common sense to run the fuck away from something way beyond their comprehension. He tried to shoo it away with a hiss and snap-sweep of his hand to the chipmunk, but it was too late.

As if the meteor had the same micro processing smarts as a Commodore 64 computer, a tendril of the boiling gunge sprang to the right, like the wiry tongue of that unfortunate chump who lost his head in *The Thing,* snaking around a tangible support to pull itself along.

The pallid frond slammed upon the chipmunk like a human hand crunching a tabletop ant. The chipmunk tried to dart away but was nowhere near fast enough to escape its fate.

"Oh, shit!" Kevin exclaimed, feeling his stomach churn to watch the chipmunk shriek in agony as the alien extension—the meteor shit—burned straight through its brown, white and black hide. It sounded like his mom frying bacon. Worse than. The substance seizing the chipmunk was corrosive, acidic, splitting skin into bloody fragments, shearing the skin away and getting down to the gristle.

Its tiny eyeballs protruded then exploded altogether. Twin bursts of gore that disgusted Kevin, yet he couldn't peel himself away from the astonishing slaughter.

Before long, the meteor shit had whittled the chipmunk down to its cerise inner frame. As if giving Kevin a final moment to reflect on what he'd just seen, the chipmunk was then tugged rapidly to the epicenter of the steam-covered muck.

Kevin inched backwards, ready to bolt out of there. Keeping his eye trained on the meteor shit to ensure it wasn't going to snap out for him, Kevin scrambled to elevate himself, then he tore off.

Faster than he'd ever been, Kevin was out of the woods in no time.

Stopping at the dirt mounts to catch his breath, his thoughts drifted from what he'd just endured to the sneering waste of sperm that was Scott Schneider.

A plan was forming.

***

Sunday, Kevin's parents had decided to sleep in instead of going to church. It had been this way for quite a while, since the entire family had grown addicted to *Ghost Host Theatre* every Saturday night, which cut off around 1:30 a.m.

Last night's dinner was great, though Kevin barely tasted it. *The Tingler* came and went in a blur, even with the expected evocations of moviegoing yesteryear from Kevin's dad. His father also liked to talk about how he'd made out with his future wife at Bengie's Drive-In, which had been playing a triple feature of *The Beast from 20,000 Fathoms, Them!* and *The Creature Walks Among Us.* Without any of those movies playing last night, the fond memories came spilling out nonetheless during the commercial breaks. His mother had giggled at it all and whipped up a batch of Jiffy Pop popcorn on the stove for their 'round midnight movie.

Kevin had played "Digital Bitch" from *Born Again* four times this morning, one, to take his mind off what he'd found in the woods, two, to stop himself from doing what he'd been thinking on doing since dashing home yesterday. Three, because the damn song was growing on him and not just because of the risqué title.

The temperature, according to the Channel 45 weatherman, Carl Spangler on last night's broadcast, was supposed to hit 75 today. Two degrees higher than yesterday. Indian summer, his dad called it, though that was just dumb, since there were no actual native tribes still situated in Maryland.

After eating a chocolate vanilla Pop Tart and making himself a glass of milk gunked by three long squeezes of Hershey syrup, Kevin left the townhouse just as he heard the floorboards from his parents' bedroom squeaking then thumping overhead. A lot of laughter from his mother accompanied by more noisy frolicking came. He knew that playful rhythm. His parents were playing grab ass first thing out of bed.

He took his Spaulding basketball with him, dribbling it a few times down the sidewalk leading from his house before carrying it the rest of the way to Streaker Court, where the community hoops and tennis courts lay.

I know the son of a bitch is going to come for me, he thought to himself, recalling the last time Kevin tried to shoot hoops by himself. Scott Schneider had made an appearance then, along with Eric Johnson and two other boys who tended to grab the court for themselves nearly every Saturday, Joey Fiorito and Danny Metcalf.

Together, they'd surrounded Kevin on the court and despite having their own basketball to start a pickup game of two-on-two, they'd swiped Kevin's ball after it doinked off the hoop rim and landed right to Joey Fiorito. After a lot of the usual name calling (Kevin remembered "Douche Mouth," "Dick Cheese" and "Raggedy Wimp" with vivid recall) prevailed with a lot of teasing to give the ball back, Scott Schneider intercepted Kevin's Spaulding and punted it to the end of Streaker. The ball had nearly been flattened by an oncoming Dodge Dart, the driver bawling Kevin out for the ball crossing his path.

Right now, the courts were empty. Not even the older people swatting fuzzy green tennis balls back and forth to the point of futility, terminating at the height of the nets instead of volleying back and forth.

Kevin took a deep breath, already picturing how this was going to go down. Assuming Scott Schneider showed up. Also, assuming he was alone, since Eric Johnson was almost always at Scott's side. Butt buddies, Kevin liked to call them underneath his breath. Kevin wasn't sure what he'd do if both came, but he'd figure it out. Ad lib it, one of his mother's go-to sayings.

He dribbled his ball a few times, the last one being a bit too hard as the basketball soared over his head. Kevin had been thinking of Scott Schneider exploding into a thousand bloody pieces.

He stood close to the basket and lobbed the ball instead of aiming it at the net. Accordingly, the ball dinged off the rim and bounced away from him a few times before rolling to a stop at the upraised corner of the court.

Kevin fetched the ball, and feeling plucky, he whirled and sprang off his feet, shooting the ball from a side angle.

"Wow," he whispered in admiration as the net swished with his basketball threading through it before bouncing to a standstill beneath the hoop.

"Nice shot, fairy lips!"

Instead of flinching and wanting to drop to the ground in surrender to his fate, Kevin grinned, his back still to Scott Schneider.

If his recent shot had been lucky, Kevin was even luckier, as Schneider was, for once, all by himself.

Kevin felt a nervous flutter inside his chest. Adrenaline chased it away, scouring Kevin's insides, telling him it was ready to serve him.

Scott Schneider had made a rare solo appearance. This was now or never.

"Gimme the ball," Schneider ordered him, his outstretched hand showing a set of grimy, uncut fingernails. Kevin glanced at his own, trimmed yesterday with the rest of his clean-up act. He'd showered a second time after getting back from the woods. He'd done so again today, as if making up for lost time.

"Eat shit," Kevin found himself saying, pressing the ball firmly against his hip. He was stunned by his unexpected boldness but loved himself for it just the same.

"Excuse me, you little cunt?" Schneider roared, the reddened flush in his cheeks telling Kevin he'd cut a nerve. A deep one he let seldom few see. "Who the fuck do you think you are, talking to me that way? Gimme the damn ball before I beat your wussy ass right here."

"You want it so bad?" Kevin sneered, for the first time feeling alive, feeling strong, feeling like he could finally stamp out this curse of abuse he'd been suffering since the end of sixth grade. On his own. The eradication would start here, with Scott Schneider. Everyone else beyond him, if they dared beat on Kevin again after today.

Kevin had caught Scott off-guard, and the latter took an unexpected step backwards.

"Easy, tiger," Schneider said, betraying the first sign of concern ever between them. Was it sudden fear? God, Kevin hoped so.

"I'm not taking your bullshit anymore," Kevin growled, feeling his thin arms fill with a need to erupt, then his hands. As if bestowed the phantom strength of long-ago titans, he cradled the basketball at his waist like a dare. *As* a dare.

"You'll always be a bitch," Scott fired back, but with half the starch of his usual aggression. "You're *my* bitch, never forget—"

Scott Schneider never got to finish that thought as he was suddenly cut off by a hard, orange sphere smelling of tire rubber. Thrust at his face with such speed he'd had no time to deflect it.

Blood spattered the basketball court and for a moment, Scott looked dazed, punch drunk as his nose gushed. His upper lip was split, also bleeding, as Kevin's basketball fell to the asphalt between them.

"Who's the bitch now?" Kevin jeered as he sprang to the right and ran like hell, leaving his ball behind

"You're fucking dead, Plympton!"

Already with a sizeable lead on Scott, Kevin poured on the speed, pounding his cleaned-up Nikes along the roadway leading out of Streaker Court. Not because he was afraid. Those days were over.

It was because he had a strategy and thus far, Scott was playing his game to a tee. So long as Schneider didn't catch Kevin, today would assuredly be Scott's last day on the planet.

An Oldsmobile was coming in hot along the main throughway, Hughes Street, well above the posted speed of 30 miles an hour. Selfish, thoughtless driving being the norm in the subdivision. The norm across the entire state of Maryland, as a matter of fact.

Kevin shifted his direction to the left to allow the fast passage of the Oldsmobile, taking another sharp cut back to the right as he crossed Hughes Street in the direction of the dirt mountains and the woods past them.

This time, Kevin avoided climbing up and down the monster mound. There was no time for it. It could mean the difference between pulling off this insane stunt or getting pounded to death, because Kevin knew, should things come to it, Scott Schneider would make good on his threat to kill him. The stakes had risen that high.

Fair enough, Kevin conceded as he thrashed his elbows back and forth to give him extra propulsion and increase the slight advantage he had on Scott.

"Goddamn pussy!" Scott roared at his back, getting close enough to make a grab. Kevin felt a slight tugging on the back of his plain gray long sleeve and for a moment, he thought he was a goner. Kevin flash-checked just enough to see the crimson smears streaked across Scott's cheeks and above his lips.

Unbelievably, Scott hesitated as Kevin blasted into the woods. The stoppage was short-lived as Kevin heard the clomping at his back resume. It had been enough for Kevin to gain some distance as the sulfur stink, hit him, then Scott Schneider.

"What's that awful smell?" Scott protested, stopping where he was. "What are you playing at here, Plympton?"

Kevin found the location of the meteor by the mauled trees, and he bounded off the trail in its direction. He took a few steps towards the bubbling morass, which seemed to increase in intensity as if sensing what Kevin was bringing to it. Like a lamb to the slaughter.

"The fuck you go, Plympton?" Schneider blared. "I'm gonna throw up all over my shoes from this stench, but not before I crush your ass!"

The yellow mire, the meteor shit, began to smoke again, as if trying to help Kevin lure Scott Schneider to it. Crouching behind the thick wedges of a pair of maple trees, he knew straight up the meteor shit was lending him a hand. If it was anything like the gooey appendage incinerating that foolish chipmunk yesterday, Kevin predicted it would come double size and double hard for Scott.

"Right here, *bitch!*" Kevin hollered, glancing at the frothy pool of beige oxidization and cracking a nod at it. In cahoots, as it were.

"Where, dammit?" Scott demanded, beginning to show signs, as he did on the basketball court, of doubt. Of outright panic. His nose had stopped bleeding, yet he looked like a clown without the white foundation palette.

Scott wheeled his head back and forth in search of Kevin, venturing closer to the meteor shit. Incredulously, without spotting it, plain as it should have been by now.

Schneider missed spotting Kevin's squatted position, another stroke of luck.

"Holy Christ!" he bellowed, finally spotting the meteor shit. His back was to Kevin.

Thus, Scott never saw Kevin spring into action, his palms thrust outwards. It was only the sound of Kevin's scurrying in his direction when Scott Schneider realized what was happening. What was going to happen to him.

For his part in it, Kevin barely felt his hands touch Scott Schneider's swinging shoulder blade. All he saw was Schneider lose his balance, pitch forward and tumble face first into the meteor shit.

"YEEEEEEEAAAHHHHHH!!!!!"

On his stomach, partially submerged inside the mordant alien gook, Schneider thrashed like a million electrodes had seized him. His voice gurgled then faltered as the unearthly skin cutting fluid seeped into his throat, scorching Scott from the inside. Kevin saw what appeared to be a dozen or so yellow extensions rise above his hated enemy, then morph into hands which pressed Scott Schneider down into its corrosive innards.

The last thing Kevin saw was Scott Schneider's skin split through his clothes, already burning off in a sweep of fire. The yellow hands, having done their job, pooled around Schneider's exposed back, eating through him. Kevin nearly screamed himself to see Scott's ribcage so quickly on display, musculature and blood dripping between the gaps.

***

"I did it," Kevin said into the tape recorder, loud as he dared. His parents were in the living room watching Marlin Perkins natter about koala bears and dingoes in the Australian outback on *Mutual of Omaha's Wild Kingdom.* "Schneider's gone. I'm not going to say how it happened. You wouldn't believe me anyway. All I know is I'm never going into those woods again. Unless there's a reason to."

As always, Kevin listened to his recount three times before rewinding it back to the beginning. Then he turned on the radio and hurriedly slammed his fingers in the appropriate places on the Philips recorder as the opening strums of Krokus' power ballad, "Screaming in the Night" lofted from 98 Rock.

Kevin kept mum with a satisfied smirk as Krokus buried his confession.

Author's Note

Friends, I put my bones into these stories.

Two of the terror tales you've just read in *Bringing in the Creeps* were hijacked from prior publications. "Galaga Dreams" first appeared in 2024 at *Punk Noir,* and "Widow," which originally haunted the 2015 anthology, *Axes of Evil II.*

In the middle of writing the other stories here, I answered a call for *Alfred Hitchcock Mystery Magazine's* "Mysterious Photograph" contest. The prompt was titled "The Cleansing of the Soles." My story earned Runner-Up and mention in *Alfred Hitchcock.* You can imagine my elation, having played Bernard Herrmann's score for *Vertigo* while whipping that little ditty up. It's my honor to share this piece with you inside *Bringing in the Creeps.*

"Age of Quarrel" recreated a real event from my metal and punk days as a teenager. Skinheads were part and parcel to slam pits and while many respected the silent moshing codes, there were a few Dave Klebans out there, one of whom was making life hell for one of our buddies of color, Rod. The Sieg Heil thing in "Age of Quarrel" was exactly how it happened in real life. I just happened to drop *The Evil Dead* into this bloody, nutty affair with a deeper message I wanted to impart.

"Lucky Burns" was incipiently the title of a failed novel I tried more than a decade ago, but with an entirely new concept. I didn't want to merely bitch and moan about author rejection here. What if the writer struggling to make a name for herself is a self-flogging firebug? Poor Audrianna was going to lose her personal war, no matter what, only to posthumously win.

If there's one story in *Bringing in the Creeps* which took everything I had, it's "Chickeerun." I was raised by Fifties kids and Boomers who taught me the culture, the music, the t.v. shows, the movies, the ways of teen life back then, even the McCarthy driven politics. I set out to make *Rebel Without a Cause* meets *American Graffiti* meets Stephen King's *Sometimes They Come Back*. This story was for all of them. When I was finally finished with "Chickeerun," I sat at my desk and spun The Beach Boys' "All Summer Long," *American Graffiti's* bittersweet fadeout tune. "I did it," I muttered aloud, and I wanted to cry with joy right there. You have no idea, friends, how much I treated "Chickeerun" as duty.

As you might infer, the *Creepshow* homage, "Meteor Shit," is my other love letter to Stephen King. As is the title of this collection, goofing on the old gospel hymn, "Bringing in the Sheaves." *Creepshow* is one of the beloveds of my life. If you come into my office, my vintage *Creepshow* 1982 theatrical movie poster is the first thing to grab you, even with all the Godzilla paraphernalia and Egyptian totems.

"Meteor Shit" is also a purge piece from my tormented life at age 12. The setting is real, the kids are authentic to the early 1980s as I knew them. Scott Schneider is very much like the mean ass son of a bitch who literally chopped me down back then, along with countless other kids at Perry Hall Middle School. Until the day came when I snapped and beat the tar out of five boys and the persecution finally stopped. "Meteor Shit" is also for John Carpenter, who redirected my entire broken course with *The Thing* '82.

Now, thank you time.

Thank you, as always, to my wife, TJ. You are my hero. You challenge me to rethink and write better, you get my marketing materials made, you brag on me and pitch me around. You have tremendous courage, and I love you beyond words. Nolan, Melissa and Nick, we both love you and hope we make you proud of what we've built together. Mom and Pop, never underestimate what a gift you are.

Thank you to Tony Anuci for giving me this forum to tell my twisted tales. A fellow metalhead, comic book hound and horror guy, this was no fluke meeting. Bless you, Tara Caribou for getting behind my three prior books, *Behind the Shadows, Revolution Calling* and *Coming of Rage.* You believed in me, you ran ads for me, you got me onto podcasts, you made me your class pet. Alaska to Maryland, we'll always be family.

Thank you to Paulette Kaler and her husband, Mark. First friends I ever had in this life. Still there, faithfully. Paulette has carried an annual Christmas tradition with me, starting at 1983's *Pet Sematary,* and every holiday since gifting me each of Stephen King's books. Later, it would include releases by his running mate, fellow Maryland homie, Richard Chizmar. Thank you, Paulette, simply thank you. Thanks also for your input on "Chickeerun." Both you and TJ turned a winner into a goddamn champion.

Thank you to the incomparable comic artist Matt Slay for turning out two ripping covers for *Behind the Shadows* and now, *Bringing in the Creeps.* You're a frigging playa, Slayman.

Horns-up to Jack Mangan of Metal Asylum and The Heavy Metal Hall of Fame. You've backed my play and championed my books with reviews and livestream interviews. You remind me of the guy I was covering metal and punk once, a *friend* to the scene, first and foremost.

Thank you, Dayton, Michael Jan, Mia, Raquel, Christopher, Richard, Dawne, Sheila ("The Danish Connection"), Kelly, Mike, Brad, Jo, Team Feinstein, MWA, Rendell, Hildy, all you rad mofos, comrades and life changers. If I missed you, I suck, but I gotta shut up sometime.

As always, *thank you,* dear friends and readers, especially those who drove for hours to attend my signings last year. I cherish you for that. I'm here because of every single one of you and because I want to stay for a very long time.